G R

A

A Highlands an... ...*e Thriller #37*

First published by Carpetless Publishing 2024

Copyright © 2024 by G R Jordan

All rights reserved. No part of this publication may be reproduced, stored or transmitted in any form or by any means, electronic, mechanical, photocopying, recording, scanning, or otherwise without written permission from the publisher. It is illegal to copy this book, post it to a website, or distribute it by any other means without permission.

This novel is entirely a work of fiction. The names, characters and incidents portrayed in it are the work of the author's imagination. Any resemblance to actual persons, living or dead, events or localities is entirely coincidental.

G R Jordan asserts the moral right to be identified as the author of this work.

G R Jordan has no responsibility for the persistence or accuracy of URLs for external or third-party Internet Websites referred to in this publication and does not guarantee that any content on such Websites is, or will remain, accurate or appropriate.

Designations used by companies to distinguish their products are often claimed as trademarks. All brand names and product names used in this book and on its cover are trade names, service marks, trademarks and registered trademarks of their respective owners. The publishers and the book are not associated with any product or vendor mentioned in this book. None of the companies referenced within the book have endorsed the book.

For avoidance of doubt, no part of this publication may be used in any manner for purposes of training artificial intelligence technologies to generate text, including without limitation, technologies that are capable of generating works in the same style or genre as the Work.

First edition

ISBN (print): 978-1-912153-52-7
ISBN (digital): 978-1-917497-00-8

This book was professionally typeset on Reedsy.
Find out more at reedsy.com

A great civilization is not conquered from without until it has destroyed itself from within.

       Ariel Durant

Contents

Foreword   iii
Acknowledgments   iv
Books by G R Jordan   v
Chapter 01   1
Chapter 02   9
Chapter 03   18
Chapter 04   26
Chapter 05   35
Chapter 06   43
Chapter 07   52
Chapter 08   60
Chapter 09   69
Chapter 10   78
Chapter 11   87
Chapter 12   95
Chapter 13   103
Chapter 14   112
Chapter 15   122
Chapter 16   131
Chapter 17   141
Chapter 18   150
Chapter 19   159
Chapter 20   167
Chapter 21   176

Chapter 22	184
Chapter 23	194
Chapter 24	202
Chapter 25	210
Read on to discover the Patrick Smythe series!	220
About the Author	223
Also by G R Jordan	225

Foreword

The events of this book, while based around real and also fictitious locations around Scotland and Rome, are entirely fictional and all characters do not represent any living or deceased person. All companies are fictitious representations. This book was produced by two wolf brothers.

Acknowledgments

To Ken, Jean, Colin, Evelyn, John and Rosemary for your work in bringing this novel to completion, your time and effort is deeply appreciated.

Books by G R Jordan

The Highlands and Islands Detective series (Crime)

1. Water's Edge
2. The Bothy
3. The Horror Weekend
4. The Small Ferry
5. Dead at Third Man
6. The Pirate Club
7. A Personal Agenda
8. A Just Punishment
9. The Numerous Deaths of Santa Claus
10. Our Gated Community
11. The Satchel
12. Culhwch Alpha
13. Fair Market Value
14. The Coach Bomber
15. The Culling at Singing Sands
16. Where Justice Fails
17. The Cortado Club
18. Cleared to Die
19. Man Overboard!
20. Antisocial Behaviour
21. Rogues' Gallery
22. The Death of Macleod - Inferno Book 1

23. A Common Man - Inferno Book 2
24. A Sweeping Darkness - Inferno Book 3
25. Dormie 5
26. The First Minister - Past Mistakes Book 1
27. The Guilty Parties - Past Mistakes Book 2
28. Vengeance is Mine - Past Mistakes Book 3
29. Winter Slay Bells
30. Macleod's Cruise
31. Scrambled Eggs
32. The Esoteric Tear
33. A Rock 'n' Roll Murder
34. The Slaughterhouse
35. Boomtown
36. The Absent Sculptor
37. A Trip to Rome
38. A Time to Rest
39. Cinderella's Carriage
40. Wild Swimming

Kirsten Stewart Thrillers (Thriller)

1. A Shot at Democracy
2. The Hunted Child
3. The Express Wishes of Mr MacIver
4. The Nationalist Express
5. The Hunt for 'Red Anna'
6. The Execution of Celebrity
7. The Man Everyone Wanted
8. Busman's Holiday

9. A Personal Favour
10. Infiltrator
11. Implosion
12. Traitor

Jac Moonshine Thrillers

1. Jac's Revenge
2. Jac for the People
3. Jac the Pariah

Siobhan Duffy Mysteries

1. A Giant Killing
2. Death of the Witch
3. The Bloodied Hands
4. A Hermit's Death

The Contessa Munroe Mysteries (Cozy Mystery)

1. Corpse Reviver
2. Frostbite
3. Cobra's Fang

The Patrick Smythe Series (Crime)

1. The Disappearance of Russell Hadleigh
2. The Graves of Calgary Bay
3. The Fairy Pools Gathering

Austerley & Kirkgordon Series (Fantasy)

1. Crescendo!
2. The Darkness at Dillingham
3. Dagon's Revenge
4. Ship of Doom

Supernatural and Elder Threat Assessment Agency (SETAA) Series (Fantasy)

1. Scarlett O'Meara: Beastmaster

Island Adventures Series (Cosy Fantasy Adventure)

1. Surface Tensions

Dark Wen Series (Horror Fantasy)

1. The Blasphemous Welcome
2. The Demon's Chalice

Chapter 01

Calgacus has got me here, thought Hamish Ferguson, taking in a view that few people got, a view that was accompanied by warm air and the sounds of a late-night city. And yet, Hamish was in the old world.

The Colosseum in Rome, during the day, was a glorious sight. But here, in the quiet, with the city busy with its nighttime activities beyond, he was presented with a whole new world that very few got to see. Maybe security guards got to see it. Possibly there were occasional tours at night. Hamish had come during the day on his first visit. But now, thanks to some relatives, he could be here, to witness something so few got to.

He sat down on the stone, his hands running across it. *How many years had it been here? A thousand? More like two thousand? More than that?* He was getting giddy now, excited, losing himself, unable to think.

The entire journey had started over twelve years ago, when he'd read about Calgacus and his defiance of the Roman invaders in Scotland. As a genealogist, he was able to trace back his lineage and found Calgacus buried within it. But from there, he was able to fan out. He'd found those who had come to Italy, those who were still upholding the tales of what had happened back then. Oh, they couldn't be sure. But it had been a slight on the country, a slight from Rome, one that had never truly been repaid.

He must have heard something behind him, for he froze on the stone seat. Slowly, he turned his head. In the shadows, something moved, skulking along. And then he saw the eyes. Everywhere in this damn place were cats. Not friendly cats, either. Not the cats that some people would pick up at home and stroke.

Hamish, however, didn't like cats. He was the one who went into a friend's house, announced proudly he didn't like cats, sat down, and would have the cat jump onto his lap. It was like the wee bastards knew it. Every time, they came for him. He wasn't having it here.

He gave a sort of shooing motion with his hands, but not too strong. These were feral cats. They might make a scrab at you. They might try to have a go, fend you off. Ideally, he would kick one. But it was a hornet's nest, wasn't it? If he upset them, who knew what could happen?

His right hand went down instinctively to a satchel hung around his neck. In here was all the research. Within the pages was all the detail. This was a folder with proper notes, not the jottings he had misplaced in the room, wherever he had them.

From this research, he found so many of them, so many relatives, and then he found the society. He was excited at the thought of it. That somewhere in this world was a group running under the radar. He wasn't quite sure what they were here to do. They had all the old symbols, symbols that he'd only seen in books, rumours of them, archaeological digs that had found half-smashed items with the symbols on them. But at their meeting, they'd proudly held them up.

Calgacus. Calgacus and Caledonia, he thought. *Caledonia.* The word rang round his head. He loved that term. The term Scotland had been hijacked. There were so many people pushing their own agendas. The flags had been hijacked. You were Scottish whether or not you wanted independence, weren't you? And yet some people would take those flags and say it was only independent Scots who could wave it. Others gripped it proudly. The flag itself buried in a greater conglomeration, the British flag. But Caledonia went back to a time when it was about his land.

He smiled, and then almost jumped as the cat walked behind him. Up on his feet, he paused, aware he'd made a sudden scuffing sound with his feet. Was there anyone here? Hamish stood, watching the cat parade along his seat, jump off the end onto the ground and then skulk away.

There'd be more of them, though. That was the thing. They were so quiet. You went to put your bag down somewhere, and one of the bloody things was there. How much did he hate the creatures—these feral cats? He didn't get them. In his Caledonia, his land, his Scotland, cats back home knew how to behave. Or, if they were wildcats, they were out in the wild. They never went walking around the city centre, taking over old historic landmarks.

He glanced around again, wondering what the place would have been like in its day. The Colosseum, the battles. The days when it used to be flooded for sea battle, or else have mock reenactments of land battles. Sometimes gladiators, one on one. The place must have been in an uproar.

He'd been to the rugby. Rugby in Scotland was a passion.

His friends, when he was younger, took him to the football, but the rugby was different. Rugby was blood and thunder. Rugby was where the real men knocked the living bells out of each other, before shaking hands and having a pint, telling each other how they'd knocked each other for six.

Even when they visited from the other parts of the UK, it was all congenial. Oh yeah, you wanted to win. But the roar that went up when both teams came out. As the match swayed from here and there, the crowds would sway, too. Hamish wondered if the Colosseum had been like that, cheering for their favourites. He remembered darker times, though, with the Colosseum.

He would not have wanted to battle here. Did anybody want to come to lose their life? Maybe some swordsmen did. Maybe some of those gladiators embraced it. But there were many people thrown in for whatever crime they'd committed. Hamish felt a shiver.

'Hello,' said a voice. It was soft, and the Italian accent wrapped it up and presented the most beautiful bundle to Hamish. He had hoped it would be her. Since he'd met them, the group had taken him to the pizzeria, taken him to other places, typically Italian places. Another restaurant, showing him a bit of Italian life.

They asked what he knew, what light he could shed in the group, what history did he know? What they told him was they had big plans, and they wanted to know if he was interested in becoming a member. Back in Scotland, he'd be a connection to the homeland, back in Caledonia.

'I see you have your satchel with you,' said her voice from the darkness.

She emerged, a petite but lovely woman, at least in Hamish's eyes. She wore black trousers with black boots underneath, and yet she stood only just over five feet tall. This perfection of womanhood wore a black crop top with a light white blouse over the top. Her hair ran down the side of her neck, ending in almost ringlets. They swayed as she swayed on her way over.

'Shall we sit?' she said.

Hamish instantly pressed his bottom on the stone and then thought should he have offered her the seat first? Should he have waited for her to sit? She had dark glasses and was practically perfect in his eyes. Studious, yet sexy.

She could only have been around thirty. Of course, he hadn't asked her. That would be rude. And he had spoken little to her. But he'd hung on her every word. He hoped he hadn't been too obvious. He would have gladly joined the group if she hadn't been in it, but her presence made it a joy.

Calgacus. The history of this great Scottish warrior. The one who defended Caledonia against the Romans. It inspired him. It drove him inside. But Maria, as he thought her name was, Maria was something else.

Hamish was approaching forty. All his life he'd been the dork. When he started growing up, being a geek wasn't cool. And then he'd been into history. He'd loved the likes of Indiana Jones, but there were none in real life, were there? There were no archaeologists who got the girl, who got to race around the world and bring back artefacts that people wowed at. It didn't happen.

You were those boring people. Studious little glasses. The girl beside you didn't have long legs. Didn't have the hair that blew in the wind, like in those films. She wasn't gutsy and yet, still, desperately, madly in love with you, despite fighting her urges because she knew you weren't that good for her.

That's what he'd hoped for in life. The work, the history, immersing himself in all of that. Discovering new things, and doing it with someone by his side who was clever, articulate, and yet also spoke to his most primal needs. Here, now in Italy, had he finally found that person?

'I can't believe you've come all the way here,' said Maria softly. Her English was good, very good, but then again, she had a connection to Scotland. She had a connection to home; most of them in the society did, if not all. They nearly all spoke English, to some degree. He lacked Italian as he'd never grown up with it, it had never been part of his family. Although, as he told them, he'd always loved pizza. He wasn't sure how that had gone down.

'Can I see it?' said Maria. Her hand went across and touched his wrist, and he always thought he would blush. Forty years old, and a woman touches your arm, and you blush. Get with it, he told himself. He lifted the bag over his head and placed the satchel on his knees.

She leaned forward to take it off him, her hand gently caressing his thigh. She lifted her sunglasses and looked up into his face. He was lost in those eyes. Brown, but a deep brown. The black of her hair, too. Almost involuntarily, his left hand swept up and brushed her cheek, pushing the hair back. She twisted slightly, almost like shying away, but then she twisted back and beamed.

'I have been watching you,' said Maria. 'I think you've been watching me.'

Hamish just blushed, but then he gave a nod.

'I spotted you the first time you arrived in the group,' said Maria. 'You have that dominance when you talk. You know what you're on about, you know,'

Hamish thought his face would burn up he was going so red. Yes, the night was warm, but he was getting excited now. He imagined this when he'd heard it would be Maria to meet him. In fact, that's why he was here.

'Meet in the Colosseum. You'll had to avoid the guards,' they had said.

There were some security guards, but they had told him how to get in, how to get up high and away from them.

'They never go up there at night. Not worth it for them, and in the shadows you'll be safe. Maria will meet you.'

Hamish had imagined this moment, not once, but several times, and now here he was, and she . . . well, she was perfect. She opened up his satchel and began looking through all the paperwork and books.

'It's all there; that's everything,' said Hamish, 'everything I've found out since I've been here. Everything I know about you, your group, the things you've told me, everything.'

'And you want to be part of us,' said Maria, putting down the satchel. Her hands went forward to his, taking them, rubbing them.

'Of course,' he said.

She stood up, took his hand, and led him over to the edge of the particular level they were on.

'Shouldn't we be careful, won't they see us here?'

'No,' said Maria, 'we're in shadow, silly; we're fine here.'

'I can't believe this,' said Hamish. 'Everything, all the people I've found, how you want to lift up Calgacus again, the things you're doing, the way you're promoting his ancestors, the way in which—'

She put a finger up to his lips. Hamish was taller than her and he had to bend slightly, as with her left hand she pulled his neck down to hers.

The next ten seconds were the most glorious of Hamish's life. His lips parted, and he felt her tongue explore, his hands by his sides, deeply tempted to grab her. Hamish hungered for her, but not wanting to rush, not knowing if this really was the time because of his lack of experience. He enjoyed the kiss. He could feel a fire burning inside of him, and as the kiss broke off, he smiled, looking at her.

Maria looked up at him, but gone was the sultry smile, gone was the look of hunger in her eyes. Now there was just a look of annoyance, like he was some sort of bug. In the brief few seconds of the rest of his life, Hamish was confused. He never fully understood women.

And now he never would, for Maria took one step forward and pushed with both her arms up into his chest. The ledge behind him didn't even reach his bottom, and so he stumbled backwards and flipped off of it. The next few seconds were filled with bemusement, and then pain, and then darkness.

Chapter 02

Susan Cunningham took her passport and placed it inside the jacket she was wearing. Taking both crutches, she marched her way through, out of customs, over to the bag collection. She wasn't sure it was a good idea being here. She wasn't sure about a lot of things lately. What she knew was she was going to do her best to enjoy it.

That's what Macleod had said. That's why he'd sent her. To get a break, to get away, to get to understand herself, and, well, maybe get a bit of a free holiday on the force. He said that she wasn't to be too snappy about returning. If she liked where she was and she wanted to take a few days, he would understand.

As she swung along on her sticks, reaching the conveyor belt of luggage, she could see people looking at her. One thing about the crutches was that everybody knew you didn't have both legs intact. She hadn't been brave enough yet to wear a skirt and display her leg. It always had trousers wrapped over it.

She'd have to get used to it though, wouldn't she? After all, this was her now. At some point, she'd have a prosthetic. It would go on the end. She stopped for a moment as the luggage belt went by.

She'd had lovely legs, she'd always thought. Sometimes men would place their hands along them. She remembered men staring at them. Susan in her life had not always dealt with her looks that well. She had let herself be used by men. She'd got herself a reputation back in the station.

But that was because she was lonely. She wanted someone. Now? Well, yes, she probably still did. But she knew better than to try to find him amongst horny colleagues. People who didn't speak to her but spoke to her body.

And that's where Perry had been a problem. He was much older than her but was very caring. Perry had been a fantastic friend through all of this. He'd been the one to charge in and probably had saved her life when the incident happened—the one that took her leg from her. But she wasn't sure that she wanted him that way. And she knew it hurt him, and yet he was still here. He was still being a friend to her.

Somebody tapped her on the shoulder. They spoke in Italian, and she'd been too distracted to understand what they'd said. She asked them in Italian to say it again.

'Yes, I'm fine,' she replied. 'I was just thinking for a moment.'

She looked down and saw her bag at the far end of the carousel, pointing it out to the man. He was going to lift it up for her. She waved her hand, insisting no. She was going to do these things herself. Susan hadn't brought a suitcase because trying to drag a suitcase when you're on two crutches didn't really work. She could manage one crutch if she was just footering about. But because she was travelling, she wanted that extra stability. It was also hard when you had the rucksack on your back.

As it came round, she grabbed the blue rucksack, sweeping a hand through the strap, swinging it directly onto her shoulder

CHAPTER 02

while she leaned on the other crutch. This is what she did. The spare crutch was dangling off her other wrist. Now having her bag, she marched off out into the outer concourse of the Leonardo da Vinci-Fiumicino Airport.

Dalcross was where she'd flown from, when she had started out. Dalcross. Why was Inverness Airport known as Dalcross and not something snappy like Leonardo da Vinci? It could have been—oh, she didn't know who—and then she laughed. Macleod-Dalcross Airport. He was becoming a celebrity, in some ways. There were rumours they wanted him to do the Christmas lights this year.

She nearly burst out laughing at that. There'd be no way Macleod would ever do that. Seoras was not one for the limelight.

Susan smiled as she continued along until she saw a card being held up by a man. It said 'Cunningham, Police Scotland' on it. Susan swung her way over and beamed at the man before her. He was maybe in the late twenties, early thirties. He had a rather dapper suit on, the cut of which suggested he was well built inside. His dark hair and his blue eyes gave him the effect of a poster boy. Susan wasn't looking for anyone, but she was quite happy to be surrounded by good-looking, intelligent people. But they'd have to be fun too. This one looked like fun.

'Hello, I'm Susan. DC Susan Cunningham, Police Scotland. How do you do?'

Then she realised that she'd said it in English. She was in Italy. She had a good grasp of Italian. Susan had studied it. There'd been parts of the family that had even been Italian. Her family had married into them and she'd spoken Italian for a fair amount of her life. And here she was, with a chance to use it. And she'd basically thrown it out the window for English.

'Hello, I'm Superintendent Matteo Lombardi. You'll be working with me on the case. I thought I would come and pick you up personally.'

'Sorry,' said Susan, looking a little embarrassed. She wanted to rub a hand through her blonde hair, but she had two sticks, which made it awkward. 'I meant to speak in Italian, but I started in English. Let's speak Italian.'

'You don't have to,' said Matteo. 'I know it's my country, but I speak good English. Italian's a struggle.'

Susan switched into Italian. 'I think it's best while we're in your country that I speak the language. I think it's best we converse that way. It'll get me greater respect amongst your colleagues. And you can also talk to them and I'll know exactly what they're saying about me.'

Matteo laughed. 'Why don't we take you to the hotel? You can settle in.'

'I'm the wrong type of girl for that,' said Susan. 'We'll dump this bag in the car and then you and I can go to the crime scene. I take it there's still a crime scene.'

'It's a national tourist spot,' said Matteo. 'Forensics moved in quickly. We've got all the details from the site, but I'll take you there anyway, so you can see what happened. I have some photographs in a brown envelope in the car. Can I take that bag for you?'

Susan put her hand up. 'I don't wish to be rude. If I need help, I'll ask. Otherwise, let me do it myself.' He was trying to help. She'd learnt never to have a go at people trying to help, because that's all they're doing.

Matteo led the way out to the car park, where Susan nearly

dropped her crutches on seeing his car. Clarissa would have loved it. It was blue and a sports edition. Some sort of coupe. Beyond that, Susan didn't really know, but it looked cool.

This Italian trip was turning out to be a good one. She had a handsome young detective with her and she was going to get to run around in a smart open-top car. She flung the rucksack onto the back seat, along with her crutches, before hopping into the passenger seat. Matteo took the car out of the car park, driving through the busy streets of Rome, making a beeline for the Colosseum. As they drove along, he asked her questions.

'How long have you worked in the police?' he asked.

'Five years now,' said Susan.

'How long a detective?'

'A year or so,' said Susan. 'I was fortunate. My detective chief inspector, he pulled me out when I wasn't getting along so well. I was working with Uniform, but I was, well, I had a bit of a reputation,' she said.

Matteo gave a smile. 'How did the injury happen?'

'I was saving someone,' said Susan, 'holding a wall up after an explosion. It came down on me. The leg was crushed and had to be taken off.'

'I'm sorry,' said Matteo. 'That must have been traumatic.'

Susan nodded. What could you say to that? It had been traumatic. It had been damn traumatic.

'I hope you've got time for some fun while you're here,' said Matteo.

'Plan on it,' said Susan. 'I expect you to point me to the best restaurants going.'

'It's still warm, too. I can take you to some of the better swimming pools. Maybe down to the beaches. Have you brought swimwear with you?'

Swimwear, thought Susan. She hadn't. If she brought swimwear, her leg would be bare. She had gone nowhere with a bared leg yet. She wasn't sure how she felt about lying on a beach.

Susan had been used to the idea of lying on a beach and people looking at her, men especially. She was comfortable with that. Except now they would look at the stump. Somebody called it 'the stump.' It wasn't a stump; it was her leg.

'Sorry, have I overstepped?' asked Matteo. 'Maybe it's a difficult subject.'

'Yes,' said Susan suddenly. 'Yes. Let's see how we get on. I have no swimsuit with me.'

'Well, if you want to,' said Matteo, 'we have plenty of shops. If it's all too public, I could find a private pool somewhere quiet, maybe fewer people.' He smiled.

'Maybe,' said Susan. He'd been kind, and he'd seen the problem. Then again, he was a detective, so he should deduce the problem.

They arrived at the Colosseum, and after parking, Susan swung her way alongside Matteo. He was able to get special passes before leading Susan into the centre of the ancient arena. Susan found her breath taken away. People had talked about it before, but now she was in the middle of it. She could see the idea of gladiatorial combat, of people cheering down at you. It was like a lot of sporting arenas in the modern day—the big ones, the vast stadiums.

'The victim was found down here, over to the side. We estimate he fell from somewhere up on that side. You can see his face.'

'Fell?' prompted Susan.

'Sorry,' said Matteo. 'Tumbled from up there. You're

thinking?'

'I'm wondering,' said Susan. 'Did he jump? Was he pushed? What did he have on him? The report said just clothing and ID.'

'That was it,' said Matteo, 'as the report stated. Nothing else. His passport. That's how we knew who he was. Well, Hamish Ferguson. From the passport, we discovered he's a genealogist. He traces lineages of people, goes into the past to find out where they came from. The idea he was somewhere like this makes sense, though I do not know what he was working on.

'We found the hotel where he was staying,' said Matteo, 'but his room had clothing in it. Nothing else. Other than toiletries. He only had a small backpack.'

'Have you been able to trace anywhere he's been?'

'Not yet,' said Matteo. 'We've put a request to the public asking for any information. But so far, we've not been able to come up with anything, but it's only been a couple of days. It's why we asked you over, to give us some help, coordinate with your people back in Scotland, in case we need to trace him, trace his family.'

'No family to trace,' said Susan. 'Only child; parents are dead. He's an academic. Few friends. Absorbed in his work.'

'Do we know what he was doing over here?' asked Matteo.

'No,' said Susan. 'I spoke to some of his colleagues in his work before I left. He said he'd been planning this trip, hadn't said about visiting anyone in particular. He was very into ancient Scotland, but they said this was probably personal more than academic. One of his friends said he had a great love of Caledonia.'

'Caledonia? What does that mean?'

'Caledonia used to be what we were called when your people

showed up. Remember the Romans came and they don't get up to the north because of the Picts. Well, Caledonia fought back before that as well. It's an old name for Scotland. Well, a part of Scotland. Like all things in history, boundaries change places. But he was very into that. I reckon he's been tracing his lineage back.'

'What lineage is there here?'

'I don't know. I'm not a historian,' said Susan. 'But it might be an idea.'

They walked around the Colosseum and then up higher into the stone stadium.

'He could have fallen from here,' said Matteo, as they stopped near the edge. 'It makes sense. I reckon it's in this general area.'

'Was he meant to be in here?'

'No,' said Matteo. 'The Colosseum was closed. None of the guards saw him come in.'

'I see nothing so far to say he was in a suicidal mood, but we don't have anybody with him either.'

'My boss believes it's an accident. He wants me to shut the case down quickly. I'm waiting for the forensic evidence to come back. More analysis. In the meantime, I want to know who the man was, what he was doing here, where he went, see if anybody had reason to get rid of him.'

'Sounds good to me,' said Susan.

'You've had a long flight. Maybe by tomorrow morning we'll have something. Why don't we have a bit of fun tonight,' said Matteo. 'I've had this case in my head for the last couple of days, so I could do with a night off. Nothing's going to change tonight.'

'Let's do that,' said Susan. 'What were you thinking?'

'Nightclub. Can you dance like that?'

'No,' said Susan, laughing. 'No, I can't. But I'll come to the club. Maybe a quiet part of it so we can talk.'

'It's still warm at night here, so you don't need to wrap up too warm,' said Matteo. 'Let me show you a good Italian night,' he said. 'Not too late. We'll have work to do tomorrow.'

'Sounds splendid,' said Susan.

As she worked her way back down the Colosseum, out to the car, Susan smiled to herself. This was turning out to be a relaxing night. Seoras was right, and he often was, wasn't he? It would do her good, being away from everyone.

Chapter 03

Susan stood in front of the hotel room mirror, staring at herself. She moved the crutches off to one side, standing on her single foot, inspecting herself up and down. The only thing that looked strange was the missing foot at the bottom. There was only one. That was an issue.

It was always one shoe. She couldn't wear stilettos, couldn't wear anything with a heel, for that matter. She was just too unbalanced. It also, by the time you swung yourself along for a day, caused a pain in the foot. So, her summer dress had a single white trainer at the bottom.

It was clean and new, hadn't been worn for long, and didn't look out of place with the dress. The dress was long, not something that Susan would have worn previously. She'd always thought she had good legs, so she would have worn a short skirt or a pair of shorts. Now, it was different.

She could feel tears coming to her eyes, as a thought went through her head that if she looked from the waist up, she could still look perfect. She'd still look good.

Susan hopped back over to the bed, collapsing on the floor beside it. Was this a good idea? She hadn't gone out much at home. And when she did, it was with the team. Or it was somewhere quiet.

Perry had been about. He was a buffer for any introductions. He could intercept people, pick up the difficult bit without her having to explain to everyone. If she struggled, he covered for her. She was now going to go out with Matteo. And Matteo, for as lovely as he was, was an unknown. She glanced at the watch on her wrist. Five minutes. She'd need to get ready.

Picking herself back up onto her good leg, she grabbed one crutch and took herself to the bathroom. She brushed her hair, staring at the mirror. This is what she would have done beforehand. Susan would have got herself ready, would have looked good for going out.

She needed to do the things she did before. This was not a stop-on-life. When it had happened, everything had been fine. She had got on with it. It was almost like a challenge. But now she could get about. Now she was working at her job. And things had changed.

Susan noticed people looked differently. People questioned you. Not out loud, but in their minds. You were broken, damaged goods. Her mind wasn't damaged. Her mind was still sharp. Macleod had said to her after the accident that he had picked her, not because she was the physically fit one to be running around. He didn't do that.

He was older, and he didn't have the strength and the charge that he used to have. But his mind was as sharp as ever, even if he struggled to work computers. He still read people, and he said that she did, too. She could still detect. He said he was sending her to Italy because she could do the job first and foremost. Secondly, because it would be an enjoyable experience for her. Thirdly, because she could actually speak Italian and fourthly, it might give her a bit of a rest.

People said she had lost a leg. But she had two. One was now smaller than the other. One was only damaged. She felt the tears underneath again, but she fought them back.

No, dammit, she was going out tonight with Matteo, and she was going to have a good evening. As she heard the door of her hotel room being knocked, Susan took the single crutch and made her way out. Opening the door, she saw Matteo in a smart white shirt that was opened wide at the top. He had neat slacks, and he looked immaculate.

'Are you ready to go? I hope you like your food.'

'I do,' she said. Susan went to follow him, and he looked beyond her, back to the bed. 'Are you taking your other crutch with you?'

'No,' she said. 'I can manage on one.'

'Excellent,' he said. He put his arm out for her.

'I don't need the help,' she said.

'It's not to help you. I just thought I would escort you. You're my guest in my country. If you had two full-size legs, I'd do the same.'

'Honestly?'

'Honestly,' said Matteo.

Susan closed the hotel door behind her and allowed Matteo to escort her along the hotel corridor. He took her on a short drive out towards the edge of the city, before he pulled up at what looked like a very family-based restaurant. A table was provided, out on a balcony, looking out over the streets.

'This is my part of Rome, where I'm from. I thought I should show you it.'

'Maybe someday you can come to Scotland. I'll show you where I'm from too.'

'I'd be delighted,' said Matteo. 'Shall we order?'

CHAPTER 03

The rest of the meal went by in a flash. Susan found Matteo easy to listen to as he told her about the sights and the sounds of Rome. He talked about growing up here, his childhood, what it had done for him, how he'd got into the force. And then, as coffee arrived after the meal, he paused. 'You haven't said much.'

'No,' said Susan.

'Tell me about you. Where you're from.'

'There's nothing glamorous about it,' said Susan. 'Council estate. School. Made the police. Four years of being that constable that everybody wanted to get into bed. Daft enough to let most of them do it. Became a detective. Lost half a leg. Now pitied by most people.'

'Is that really how you see yourself?' asked Matteo.

'Well, it's the truth, isn't it?'

'You work for a DCI. That's how you say it, isn't it? Macleod?'

'Seoras Macleod.'

'I heard he's well known in Scotland.'

'Seoras is, well, he's quite the detective. He's a bit of a media— well, not star, because he doesn't enjoy being in front of cameras.'

'No, I did a little research looking at footage from former cases, when I heard you were coming over to see if I could spot you. There was a redhead woman.'

'Hope. Hope McGrath. Detective Inspector. She's my boss. DCI Macleod is her boss.'

'The media likes her.'

'She has the problem that she's too good looking a woman. They attribute everything to her looks. She's much better than that,' said Susan.

'Maybe you are, too. If this DCI Macleod picked you, he

must have thought you were good. No, I'm serious. He doesn't sound like a man who just picks anyone.'

'Are you flirting with me?' asked Susan suddenly.

Matteo looked hurt for a moment but then he rounded. 'I'm not. You come to my country; you obviously have trauma—that's how you put it. To take advantage of that wouldn't be right. So, I'm not flirting with you. But I see someone who doesn't value herself as she should. I don't know you well, but you don't talk about what you do, except to tell me how some men would want to get you into bed.

'That's not how you talk to someone. Some of these cases you help solve. You told me you held up a wall to save someone's life and paid for it. That makes you someone I want to know,' said Matteo. 'Not some woman, not someone I want to get close to in that sense, but someone I want to know. I joined the police force to help. When I see people who help, I want to know them.'

Susan smiled and sat back in her chair. She sipped her coffee, constantly smiling back at Matteo on the other side. He pushed nothing after that statement, but whisked her off to a nightclub as the day got darker.

They sat in the corner, and Susan struggled with everyone walking past, especially when somebody spotted she had one foot. To have a crutch, or to have an injury was okay, but to have a missing foot seemed to cause more attention. Matteo, realising her shame, offered to take her back to the hotel. He seemed distracted though, especially after they'd gone into the nightclub where speaking was difficult. He was now lost in his own thoughts, and Susan wondered what was getting at him.

'I'm fine, Matteo. But there must be somewhere that does

coffee.'

'It's two in the morning. It's Rome. I will find somewhere where coffee is served,' said Matteo. Back in the car, he zipped in and out of a few streets before parking at a little cafe that was still open. They sat down outside at a table on the street. Coffee was served and Susan saw they weren't the only ones. There were several other clientele, usually in pairs.

'So why do you want coffee now?'

'You switched off. In the nightclub, you switched off.'

'They're terrible places to talk. I should have thought.'

'You were somewhere else. Where?' asked Susan. For a moment, Matteo looked a little taken aback, but then he relaxed again into that gentle demeanour he had.

'Well, if you must know, I'm worried about our investigation.'

'Why?'

'I don't think it's a simple matter. A British tourist, in what is one of our top attractions. It's bad to have a tourist die in a top attraction. Even worse to have them murdered.'

'But it seems like he fell.'

'We know he fell,' said Matteo, 'but we don't know if he was pushed.'

'Hold up a minute,' said Susan. 'You see, you're telling me that the evidence says he tumbled. He went backwards off wherever on the ledge. You have indications he fell, and that's how he died. There's nothing to say he was pushed. We have nothing at the moment to say there was anyone else with him. He has come into the Colosseum at night, secretly.'

'This is true,' said Matteo, 'but you also said it. He doesn't look like someone committing suicide. There's no note, there's no explanation. Why do it here? Why do it in Rome? Why not kill himself back in Scotland? Certain people will want this to be an accident. I understand that.

'I understand that our tourist people, they want it to be an accident. Tragic accident, but an accident. You can wipe it off. There's no dark side to that. It's just an accident and maybe they put up more signs; maybe they say, careful here, careful there, but it moves on and nobody gets excited. If somebody is murdered . . . then the people get excited. Then tourists think about things twice. But why was he murdered?'

'But we don't know he's been murdered,' said Susan.

'Your boss, Macleod, does he ever have a hunch?'

'Oh yes,' said Susan. 'Sometimes he knows who did it before he's even got any evidence. He reads people very well.'

'I don't have hunches like that, but I work in this city. I have seen certain things. There's a bigger picture here that Hamish Ferguson may be part of,' said Matteo.

'What does your boss say about it? Inspector Ricci. I take it I meet him tomorrow?'

'Inspector Ricci would like this to go away as well. He doesn't want to have a murder of a foreigner. Paperwork, everything else. He wasn't keen on you coming over, but I insisted.'

'So, you could get a different view; so you would have good connections with any work that had to be done in Scotland.'

Matteo looked away for a moment, as if he was considering what she said. But surely that was the reason.

'Yes,' he said, gently nodding his head. 'Yes, of course, for the communication and things like that.'

'Is there something you're not telling me?' asked Susan.

'I'll be honest,' said Matteo. 'Yes, but I'm not ready to tell you. It might make me sound crazy. It might make me bring you into something you shouldn't be in. I need more evidence, and I also need you to be untainted.'

CHAPTER 03

'Untainted?' said Susan, suddenly. 'I don't follow you.'

'I need you to see everything *cold*. Is that how you say it in English? Approach something *cold*? Not having seen it before?'

'Yes, that's right,' said Susan.

'And also, if I'm wrong, I want you to enjoy being over here. I want you to have a good time. You've had a hard time recently. I can see that.'

'But I'm here to do a job. And if that means helping you, that means helping you. It's not a jolly,' she said. *Jolly* was said in English, and Matteo looked at her.

'Don't know how to say it in Italian,' said Susan, suddenly breaking into English. 'Jolly, freebie. Holiday? On company expense?'

Matteo laughed. 'Maybe you deserve a bit of that,' he said in English. 'Either way, I want you to have a good time. And you'll help me. Trust me.' He looked at his watch. 'You should have got an early night after your travels.'

'Thank you,' said Susan, standing up. 'What time will you be picking me up in the morning? Nine? Or do you start a bit later, at ten?'

'The inspector won't be seeing you until half eleven. Maybe I'll pick you up about half ten.'

'I'm going to pop into the swimming pool in the morning. Just the hotel one. It'll be my first time. Pick me up after that. So, half ten.'

'Come then. Let's get you home.'

Yes, he was nice. He was friendly. He was good to talk to. And she was going to swim tomorrow morning. When she got into the car, she hoped and prayed that the hotel had swimsuits of some sort because she wasn't ready for a bikini.

Chapter 04

Susan had been rather disappointed in the hotel's small shop. There were no swimsuits. Clearly, they were marketing towards a younger end of the market and not someone who was there to go swimming. Instead, she'd had to pick out a bikini, which made her feel like she should look more glamorous and made her feel that her half leg was evident to everyone. Of course, it was evident. It wasn't there. But this made it even more clear.

Susan had taken a towel and the rest of her gear down to the changing rooms beside the pool. But when she stepped out, the crutch in one hand, she could see the stares. People turned away if they saw her look over, but they soon turned back to pity her.

She slipped into the water quickly, leaving her crutch at the edge of the pool. It was easy to stand up, float in the water, and while her legs were underneath it, it was easy for people to forget that she was different. It wasn't so easy for her to forget.

And as she stood there, she wondered about swimming. How do you swim with one leg? Walking had been different, but she'd been successfully walking for quite a while now with the crutch. And when she got her prosthetic, walking would be similar.

Swimming never would. She would never swim again like she had before. You didn't get a prosthetic leg in the swimming pool; you took it off. This would be a place where she was always exposed as being different. But she was different, wasn't she?

She decided to try some breaststroke. Susan pushed off from the wall, glided forward, but it felt different. It felt like something just wasn't happening. And yet she was going forward. She was swimming. She got to the end, turned round, and tried the front crawl. Again, different. Not the same power coming from her legs. Well, leg. And the rhythm, the timing of it. It felt awkward. It felt different, too.

She never realised how much her legs had worked together as a pair. She never thought about it. And then suddenly one wasn't the same. It was like you were unbalanced. Not that you couldn't make it work. You just weren't making it work the same way. It didn't feel right.

Susan went on to her back and felt the same again. Eventually, she hauled herself out of the pool and sat in the spa. A man in his thirties came and sat down in the spa beside her. He conversed a few words in Italian. She felt he was flirting with her but she wasn't in the mood for it. Yet she was polite and she spoke back in Italian before hauling herself out of the spa to return to the pool.

She had called it quits when she caught his look when he saw the half-leg. He didn't hide it at first, an almost disgusted look of horror. *Well, screw him*, thought Susan. She plonked herself back in the pool and moseyed about, swimming a few lengths. She'd have to get back into it properly, learn how to deal with this, how to be like a fish again in water.

She held herself on the side of the pool and looked up to see Matteo arriving in the swimming pool area. He'd taken his shoes off and was walking across on his bare feet, making him look rather strange with his suit on. He smiled as he saw her.

'Good for you,' he said.

'Not been without its difficulties,' she said in Italian. 'But I've done it. They didn't have a swimsuit in the shop. I had to get a bikini.'

'Well done,' he said. His tone wasn't patronising at all. Susan smiled.

'Why are you here?' she asked. 'You said half ten.'

'I did, but the inspector has pulled our meeting forward with him. I suspect he had something cancelled. You'll need to come along now.'

'Okay,' she said. He stepped away to one side and sat down in a chair by the pool, while Susan half hopped and swam over to the pool edge, placing her hands on the side. She hauled herself out and looked to where Matteo was sitting down.

'You couldn't reach me the crutch, could you?' she asked.

Matteo nodded, grabbed her crutch and brought it over to her. He went to give her a supportive arm, but she waved him away.

'No, no, I'll have to do it myself,' she said. Between the crutch and her good leg, she forced herself up onto her foot.

'Do you mind if I say I'm glad you got the bikini?' said Matteo. He was looking at her now, his eyes scanning her from head to foot. She smiled back. There was no sign from him of a disgust or of shock at the stump.

'You look quite stunning,' he said.

'Thank you.'

CHAPTER 04

Susan noted it was a genuine compliment and he didn't seem to look for anything more. She got a towel and dried herself down. She told him she'd head into the changing rooms and meet him in the lobby in about twenty minutes. Matteo nodded, quietly left, but he had one glance back at her. She liked that. He was being very polite, but he certainly wasn't insincere. *Better than that arsehole in the spa,'* she thought.

It took the full twenty minutes for her to change, get to her room, sort herself out, and get back down to the lobby. As she did so, she was on both crutches again. Matteo stood up, approaching her.

'Are you sure you don't want me to give you a hand?'

'It's a full day,' she said. 'At the moment, I need them for the full day. When I get back, hopefully, I'll get a prosthetic. I'll learn to walk without them. But at the moment, I need them. My arms get tired. Everything gets tired if I'm just working on one arm.'

'Okay,' he said. 'I can't promise that my boss will be as enamoured by you as I am.'

'He doesn't like women?' asked Susan.

'He'll ask why they sent you over. Not to you, but to me. He'll ask why we've got an amputee. He's not very fair. Ricci is not that well invested with manners. He does know his stuff, police-wise, but he's not the best at dealing with other people.'

Susan swallowed hard. Well, she'd just have to deal with it. They drove to the police station on what was another bright day. Susan felt hot. She had a light jacket on, along with a t-shirt. Her foot had a white trainer, along with white cotton trousers. She'd sewn up the leg where it now stopped.

She did her best to march into the police station, looking as confident as possible. But in truth, something inside of Susan was churning away at her. Matteo had been lovely, but this is where they would tell her she didn't belong, tell her to get her legs sorted.

As she was about to skip into the office and be taken into the meeting, her mobile phone went. She saw the name, and almost welcomed it.

'Two minutes, Matteo,' she said, 'it's the boss.'

'How's things?' asked Macleod as Susan picked up the call.

'Oh, the case. Seoras, not convinced that this was an accident, but got a good bit of investigating to do before we can draw proper conclusions.'

'I hope it's not been all work and no play.'

'I was taken to dinner last night, so no. It's going okay.'

'Good, because it's boring back here. Clarissa's off on one, as ever, but Hope's quiet at the moment, so I'm quiet, and I'm stuck, stuck adding up numbers as ever, passing back memos and stuff. Should have gone out there myself.'

'Well, thank you for it,' she said. 'I think it's going to do me good.'

'Just take care. And find out what happened to him.'

'Of course.'

Susan put the phone away inside her jacket and marched into the meeting room that Matteo had pointed out to her. When she entered, the conversation was hot inside. It wasn't like the station back home. Maybe because the team was more chilled. You could get agitated at times, but generally it was quite civil. Here, she was surrounded by mainly men. There was a single woman on the far side who was eyeing her up with suspicion. But as Susan entered, she knew that a lot of eyes were cast upon her.

'Morning,' she said in Italian.

She sat down as the conversation returned to what they were talking about. The conversation was about Hamish Ferguson. There seemed to be a row going on about what had happened to him. Matteo was giving as good as he got from his boss, his boss insisting that this was an open-and-closed case. The man had simply fallen.

Matteo said that he didn't have all the evidence to say that. Forensics were backing him up but also saying how difficult it was to prove anything. The boss, Inspector Ricci, then laid into forensic about doing their job, what Susan found a little unfair. Jona never told you what wasn't there. She just told you what she saw, what she believed could be inferred. And to what degree it could be inferred? Ricci was demanding explanations from almost all of these people. He suddenly turned to her, staring at Susan.

'Well, Detective Constable Cunningham,' he said. 'Welcome to our country. What is your opinion?'

'I may only have just got here,' said Susan. 'But from the evidence yesterday, it's a bit too quick to decide whether or not he committed suicide. Or whether there was foul play.'

'To bring you up to date,' said Ricci. 'Forensic has said this morning that there's another set of DNA on his lips. I believe he was out the previous night with a woman. She scorned him, and that's why he committed suicide. It all ties up. It's a good story. He doesn't seem to have had any other reason to be there.'

'Nor did he have a reason to commit suicide,' said Matteo. 'We need to find out who this DNA belongs to.'

'The longer we string this out, the more it becomes a story We don't need a story,' said Ricci. 'We don't need the media hanging on to this.'

'But we need to solve it,' said Matteo. 'What do you say, Cunningham?'

'Well, sir,' said Susan in Italian. She wasn't sure if they still addressed seniors as sir or not, unlike back home. But it couldn't help to butter the man up a bit. 'It seems to me that that's something that needs answered.'

'How do you intend to do that?' asked the inspector.

'We need to look into his time here. We need to find out where he's been, see if he's been connected with a woman or indeed a man. We're not sure what his taste in a partner is,' said Matteo.

'I believe Matteo's correct,' said Susan. 'We need to track him down. We've got some loose contacts. Find out where he went.'

'That could involve a lot of work,' said Ricci. 'You're going to have a couple of days and we'll call it quits. If you find nothing suspicious, we'll tag this down as an unexplained fault.'

Susan went to object, saying they needed to do more than that. But she saw Matteo nod his head, simply, and under the table, his left hand was showing a sign that said stop.

'Thank you,' said Susan. 'We'll do our best to come up with something.'

'If there's anything there,' said the inspector.

Susan stood up with her crutch and went to leave, with her tail moving past her. But she heard a shout from the inspector.

'Can I have a word a moment, Cunningham?' he said.

Susan turned round. 'Of course you can.' And she approached his desk at the top of the room. He waited until everyone had left, including Matteo.

'Why are you here?' he asked.

'Because you requested help. Matteo requested assistance.

To setup communication lines and to do some of the work in Scotland if you needed it.'

'But why are you here? We don't need you here. It's a death we could investigate.'

'You put a call in to us asking for assistance. We came,' said Susan. 'We didn't push to come. We were requested.'

'And he sent you. You're . . .' He looked down at some paperwork. 'Your Chief Inspector Macleod sent you. Why?'

'How do you mean?'

'I mean, look at you. Are you fit for duty? You're not going to be able to run. How are you going to tackle a suspect?'

'You may find that he has sent me because of my brains, not my body.'

'Don't get in the way, whatever you do. Okay? I don't want this becoming a farce. The media will be all over it, anyway. It's at the Colosseum, this is the height of the tourist season, and we've got a death. They'll want to blow it up out of all proportion. I don't want you to be the cause of that.'

'I won't, sir,' said Susan. 'I'll investigate thoroughly. I'll produce my conclusions to you. I am on your turf—your rules, your ways. I will bring what I've got.' She tapped her head. 'I will tell you what is what, as I see it, and you will do as you do.'

'Good,' said Ricci. 'We understand each other then.'

'If I may ask,' said Ricci, with a slightly sleazy look to his face, 'Your Macleod. He kept you on after the problem . . . because he likes the look of you?'

Susan smiled, but it wasn't friendly. 'Seoras Macleod would keep no one on because of how they looked. He keeps them on because they are part of his team, and he knows they contribute. I'm here for a reason. He thinks I'm the right person. What's missing from me may be very obvious, but there's a lot missing from other people. Maybe you don't get to see that. Good day, sir.'

Susan turned on her heel and swung her way back out of the office. She closed the door behind her. She saw Matteo standing close by.

'You okay?' he asked.

'Well, I get why you don't like him,' she said. 'Shall we go?'

Chapter 05

As Matteo and Susan got to the car, Matteo reached for his mobile phone. She heard him speaking to what she thought was the forensics department and when he finished the call, he was smiling.

'We've been going through some of the rubbish around the Colosseum, looking at the bins close to where Ferguson may have entered. Some of the rubbish they ran a DNA check on. There was one map that had ringed areas on it. Nothing particularly unusual, but as he was a tourist, we thought it was worth checking. Of course, it was amongst lots and lots of other pamphlets and bits of rubbish. Turns out the hunch paid off, though. Because it was a map. A map that had ringed areas on it, and it was ripped up. It's got his DNA on it, though.'

'Just his,' said Susan.

'Only his we can identify. Well, that means he had enough, and he did commit suicide, or . . . well, he was getting rid of it for a reason.'

'And what's been ringed?'

'The Sistine Chapel. St. Peter's Square. There's the Vatican Secret Archives as well. Outside the Papal City, there's Trajan's Column. The Capitoline Museums. The Basilica Giulia and the Roman Forum. So, it's his holiday, by the looks of it.'

'Why would he go to these places?' said Susan.

'Let's go back into the office a minute and think about this.'

The pair drove to Matteo's office. He had a small separate office, similar to what Hope had back in Inverness. Outwith that office, a small group of people were working. They all nodded at Matteo as he entered. Susan followed him into his office and he gave her a chair to sit on while he sat himself behind the computer.

'The Sistine Chapel's an obvious one,' said Matteo. 'Everybody comes to look at it. St. Peter's Square is another one. If you get a chance, see both of them but they are very tourist-sought locations.'

'The Sistine Chapel, I get. St. Peter's Square. But you said the Vatican Secret Archives,' said Susan.

'That is different, and it is very secret,' he said. 'Maybe he was planning on getting access. He's a genealogist.'

'He was,' said Susan. 'Maybe he was looking to trace an ancestor through.'

'Well, that makes sense.'

'What about these other places? Trajan's Column. What's that about?'

'Trajan's Column is from Emperor Trajan's Dacian Wars. It represents Rome's northern campaigns of the time.'

'Well, if he was looking at things about Scotland, maybe it makes sense,' offered Susan.

'It could do. The Capitoline Museums have lots of relics from times, some of them from further north, so there's a possible link there to what he was working on,' said Matteo. 'The Basilica Julia, however, has lots to do with prisoners. It's a jail.'

'But he's looking in there,' said Susan. 'This smacks of someone actually looking for history, or someone that thinks history is there,' she said. 'Especially when you bring in the Vatican Secret Archives. I mean, he wasn't going to get in, was he?'

'Not unless he knew some powerful people,' said Matteo.

'So, let's assume he doesn't, looking at where he's staying. I mean, if you're coming over and you know some powerful people, they're going to help put you up somewhere stylish.'

'Unless he's flying under the radar,' said Matteo.

'Trust me, I looked at him back home. This guy doesn't fly under the radar. He is a geek, a professor, Mr History. It's what he's into. Genealogy, names, lineages. This is what he does. I don't think he's here to cause a problem. He's here to investigate the past.'

'So, we need to understand,' said Matteo, 'what Scottish history he's looking at and how it relates to Rome.'

'And do it in about three days,' said Susan. 'It's not happening, is it? I mean, this guy's been working on this for years. We haven't even got any of his notes.'

'Maybe we could look at his papers. Maybe there's . . .'

'I did a scan of titles. It's quite wide-ranging. I think this is personal because he doesn't seem to have travelled like this before. He's gone to symposiums; he's gone to conferences. When I looked into his history and I spoke to his colleagues back home, he worked like many academics. But this is a trip by himself. The university he worked at didn't pay for this.'

'We need to know why he was here,' said Matteo. 'We need to understand where he was coming from. How can we do that? You're saying that his official work isn't leading you there.'

'It didn't. It didn't at all,' said Susan. 'What about his hotel room?'

'They've gone through it. They found nothing.'

'Can we go take a look? Sometimes you don't know what you're looking at,' said Susan.

'Well, there's nowhere else we're going at the moment, is there?' said Matteo. 'I guess so.'

Susan and Matteo walked back down to the car outside the station and soon they were whipping across town. *Yes*, thought Susan, *Clarissa would love this car.* She gave her hair a shake, letting it blow out in the wind generated by the car. She caught Matteo looking at her.

'Watch the road,' she said.

'I think the swim did you good.'

'You did me good,' said Susan. 'But some idiot made a comment when I was in the jacuzzi. Not a nice one.'

'You know you'll get that. Understand what you are.'

'And what am I?'

'Intelligent, good-looking woman. And hopefully a talented detective,' said Matteo. 'I don't know if that's true yet, but we'll find out.'

Susan smiled at him. She kept her eyes on him as he turned back to the road, and she saw his face grimace again. Something was ticking through his mind he wasn't happy about. He'd spoken to her that night, but he would not tell her in case it tainted the way she was looking at the case. She respected that, so she decided not to push him.

The hotel that Hamish Ferguson was staying in was not a salubrious one, but it was a hotel. It was very basic, and probably very affordable. Matteo spoke initially to the owner who threw a bit of a fit, saying that the police had been here and been through it all. He had shown them to the room where

Hamish Ferguson had stayed. They had swept it; they had looked at it.

'I appreciate that,' said Matteo. 'But we have our Scottish colleague with us. She needs to see the room.'

'Why have you got a Scottish detective with you? Why do they need to see the room? What am I? An international tourist destination? You don't need this. I'm going to make a complaint. She can piss off.'

The conversation was in Italian. The man clearly thought that Susan wouldn't understand. However, she turned to him politely and said, 'I'm sorry to inconvenience you, sir, but I will not piss off. I will see that room. Please do as my colleague asked.'

The man's face fell. He hurried off to get a key card for the room. Leading them down through a passageway, he came to a door that was already open. Inside was a maid changing the bed.

'Your people have been through already. I don't know what you expect to find.'

'I don't know what I will find,' said Susan. 'I'll tell you when I've got it.'

The hotel manager disappeared out the door, leaving them in the company of the room-maid. She looked away from them and began changing the bed. Susan, using her crutches, swung her way round the room, checking drawers and found everything to be empty. The room was in change over. If it had been changed over already, what could she find? The room was uninteresting, bland, and clearly for a budget traveller. It was a shot in the dark, but she turned to the maid and asked, 'I don't suppose you were here when Hamish Ferguson was staying, a Scottish man?'

'The last two weeks,' said the woman. 'I don't get a break during this time of year.'

'So you remember the man who stayed here in this room?'

'Yes,' she said, 'but he didn't stay in this room.'

'What do you mean, "he didn't stay in this room?"'

'In the middle of the night, there was a problem. You see, he was staying in the room next door.'

'Okay. Why did you move him?' asked Susan.

'There was a fault with it. The rooms are interchangeable. See? That door there,' said the maid, pointing to a door that would lead into the room next to it. Susan swung her way over, but the door wouldn't open.

'It's locked,' said Susan.

'Yes. I've had people in here, so we've locked it. The other room, it can't be used. There's damp coming down one of the walls. Water leaks in.'

'Can you let us in?' asked Matteo.

'Of course,' said the maid.

Susan was bemused. 'Why haven't forensics looked in that room, Matteo?'

'Because forensics don't know about it,' said Matteo. 'I don't know about it.' He turned to the maid. 'How come the police don't know that Hamish Ferguson was staying in there?'

'I don't know,' said the woman. 'It happened during the night.'

'Does your owner know?' asked Matteo.

'He knows nothing,' said the woman. 'He doesn't run the place. That man only came in when the police were here, and then he's been staying since because we've had the press all over us.'

'And this move happened before the man went missing?'

CHAPTER 05

asked Matteo.

"Yes, he knows nothing about it."

'Well, this could be interesting then,' said Susan.

She opened the door, once the maid had unlocked it and could smell the dampness. There was indeed water running down one side of the bedroom, but the bedsheets were still on. Susan walked around, pulling open the drawers, but they were all empty. It was like the room had been cleared out, which, of course, it had.

Hamish Ferguson would have moved next door with all his stuff. The bedclothes obviously remained. Susan went down on her knees, finding it awkward not to tip over without the extra stabilisation of her lower leg. But she lay there, head to the ground, staring around.

'You might tell me what you're doing,' said Matteo.

'Well, I've checked all the drawers. There's nothing in there. I'm seeing if anything from a different eye level might strike me as odd.'

She scanned around, and then underneath the bed, she could see a slight bulge of the springs. She pulled herself forward with her arms, then rolled onto her back and pulled herself under the bed.

'Matteo,' she said, 'I need you to lift the duvet and the mattress. There's something under there.'

Matteo lifted the mattress. 'There's a book there. It's like a notebook,' he said.

'Have you got gloves?' asked Susan.

'Of course,' said Matteo, putting his shoulder to the mattress while he put gloves on. Taking hold of the notebook he started opening it and showing the pages to Susan.

'This is his diary, or at least his information sump, where

he's been, everything he can find out about it. And this goes back; this goes back to Scotland,' said Susan.

'I'll have to let forensics take a look.'

'Not yet, you don't.' Susan took out her mobile phone. She let Matteo turn every page, taking a photograph of each one, after which Matteo put it inside a zip bag, labelling it for forensic.

'So,' said Susan, 'I think we might learn a bit. There's a lot of reading here. I think it's time to sit down, and drink, and do that reading.'

'It's going to get hot soon. Why don't we go back to your hotel and do it? Sit at the side of the pool.'

'Why do you want to do that?' asked Susan.

'Because if you're not here, this goes back into the office. And we all sit around the rather drab office. You're here. I can say we went to your room. Go to your place. And that means sitting by a pool, doing our work. You don't need to be a detective to work out what I'm doing,' he said.

No indeed, thought Susan. Susan began looking through some of the notes on her phone. 'It's best if I read this document,' said Susan.

'Why? Just because it's British.'

'No,' said Susan, 'because the way it's written, lots of abbreviations. I'll understand them in English. Don't think you will.'

'Go on then. Let's drive back and you can tell me what you discover.'

Susan nodded, moved through the next room to thank the maid, and told her to close it up. She would leave Matteo to get forensics back and see if there was anything else they could discover.

Chapter 06

Susan Cunningham lay back and looked across the pool in front of her, and beyond to the Rome skyline. It was a city and a half to be in, and the hotel where she was staying was excellent. Macleod had recommended it, although she wasn't sure he'd ever been to Rome. She also wasn't sure what budget it was on, but then maybe things were different when you went away from the UK. You could say you couldn't find a room; you could justify slightly higher prices. As she lay back on the recliner by the pool, she had to remind herself she was actually working.

One reminder of that was Matteo, sitting in a chair close by. Between the two of them was a small table. Susan had ordered drinks, non-alcoholic of course, for she was working. Work wouldn't pick up the tab for any alcoholic ones. Of course, Macleod didn't go for alcohol, but she didn't feel she could hold it against him. Not when he'd sent her away from everyone else, working, using her brain, getting involved, but having a little space.

She had purchased a bikini in the hotel shop. Finding a swimsuit that would fit her had proved impossible. Feeling the way she did about having her leg exposed, Susan wasn't too sure about sitting out here beside the pool. Matteo had been encouraging though, and now here she was, albeit with a t-shirt on.

Back in the day, she wouldn't have had a problem lying here. There would be no self-consciousness rearing in at the back of her mind, telling her that there was something different about her. He had been so kind, complimenting her on the way she looked when she first sat down on the recliner.

The long white t-shirt had almost come down far enough to reach the top of her short leg. If she'd worked it right, because of the size of the t-shirt, she could have tucked her leg inside of it. It looked as if she was simply cross-legged.

But Matteo put her at ease. He'd also encouraged her to get reading the book that she'd photographed. It was now a series of images on her tablet.

Her short leg was sticking out from under the t-shirt. The horrible end of it, as she thought of it, on show. And sure, a few people stared as they went past. She could handle it. She was being herself.

If she'd got a prosthetic, there would still be times like this. Maybe that would have been at the back of her mind. Maybe this fear raced through it. But the overriding fear was, would she be able to attract a man again?

After all, Susan was still young. And while she'd had her fill of cheap one-night stands with officers from the station—all her supposed boyfriends she'd picked up—she hadn't given up on a proper one. Somebody she should be with, but it would be somebody who would catch her unawares, unsuspecting. Somebody she just fell in love with instead of trying to haul in.

Susan studied the book in front of her on the tablet, flicking through the pages. Hamish Ferguson was a strange sort in some ways but she was engrossed in what he was saying. Maybe that was helping. Maybe that was taking her mind off her leg. During the day, it was okay because it was covered. But here, the scar, the disfigurement, was evident.

'How much have you read of it?' asked Matteo. 'You know I'm waiting.'

'We agreed,' Susan said, 'didn't we, I would read it since it was in English? And it was talking about several places that you wouldn't be familiar with.'

'I agreed that when I thought you would actually read it instead of laughing, lying there, sipping down your drink and enjoying yourself,' said Matteo as he grinned at her.

'I am enjoying myself,' she said, 'but don't worry, I'm working as well.'

'I'll wait,' he said. 'In fact, I'll go for a walk. I'll come back in half an hour, if that's okay.'

'Of course,' said Susan. She watched him as he departed the poolside. He was young, like her, a touch, just a touch older, intelligent. But what was drawing her to him was he was very kind. He seemed to appreciate her dilemma, her issues. But, everyone else had been encouraging from Hope to Perry. Perry, who had been so kind. But he was older. Perry wasn't the kind she went for. She liked a good-looking man.

You are so vain, said Susan to herself. *So vain*. She felt bad thinking that about Perry. He'd been so good. But she'd been wary because clearly he'd become smitten.

After half an hour, Matteo was good to his word and arrived back at the poolside. He got another couple of drinks from the bar and then sat down on the edge of Susan's recliner. At one point, it looked to tip, Susan reaching out with her hands, catching herself on his shoulder. She laughed. *It was good to laugh*, she thought.

'So, have ye got anywhere?' asked Matteo. 'Or am I going to wear off the tread of my shoes?'

'Shut up,' said Susan. 'And listen! His notebook says it all starts with Calgacus and the Roman invasions when Calgacus defended Britain, or more accurately, Caledonia. Calgacus was an ancient Caledonian chieftain. And it looks like Hamish is a descendant.'

'That's a long way back,' said Matteo. 'Is he sure?'

'He's very sure,' said Susan. 'You see, Hamish was a genealogist. He'd worked hard on this, from what I can tell. He certainly believed it.'

'Is there one particular location he mentions?' said Matteo. 'He had a good wander around when he was over here.'

'Well, we saw the map, but he's talking about Trajan's Column, the Capitoline Museums, and the Basilica Julia.'

'Well, Trajan's Column depicts scenes from Emperor Trajan's Dacian Wars,' said Matteo. 'I don't remember ever hearing about Calgacus, though.'

'Well, Calgacus was defeated,' said Susan. 'So, no wonder. This is Italy. You will not go on about who you've vanquished. Especially if they were seen as an upstart. People from the edge of civilisation.'

'That's true,' said Matteo. 'The Capitoline Museums, they hold lots of artefacts. So maybe he was checking there. But the one I don't get, the Basilica Julia in the Roman Forum. That's basically a prison. Maybe we brought back captives, but I don't remember them being mentioned.'

'He's been here for over a month,' said Susan. 'That's how the log for here goes. But he's been doing this research for years.'

'Have you read it all?' asked Matteo.

'No. I'm getting towards the later sections, the more recent stuff.'

'Do you want me to leave you alone again, then?'

'No,' said Susan. She looked around. 'It's pretty empty now by the pool.'

'Well, we are into late evening. Most of us find it quite cool.'

Susan stopped for a moment. There was indeed nobody around the pool, and she noted she was the only one in some sort of swimming attire.

'You feeling the chill?' asked Susan.

'I was going to get coffee,' said Matteo. 'Do you want to get changed?'

Susan was feeling no chill. In fact, the temperature was glorious to her.

'Do you know what the temperature is?' she asked.

'I think it's seventeen degrees centigrade. Something like that.'

'Blimey, Matteo,' said Susan. 'This is our summer back home. You know that? I'm fine as I am,' she said proudly.

Both legs could now be seen beyond her t-shirt, and she was feeling no shame about it. It helped that Matteo was sitting where her leg would have been. He didn't have any sort of worries or fears about being close to the leg. Others had. Others trod around it, so to speak. But Matteo seemed to embrace the way Susan was. She liked that.

'I'll talk quietly, but I think we're okay, aren't we?'

'I think so,' said Matteo.

'Right. Section here talks about . . . wow! He's talking about a secret society in Rome that he's met, a society dedicated to Calgacus.'

'In what way?'

'Well, he's saying that Trajan's Column was erected in 113 AD, so that's thirty years, he says, after the battle of Mons Graupius, which is one that Calgacus was involved in.'

'I don't know about that,' said Matteo, 'but the scenes in it are from Emperor Trajan's Dacian Wars. As I remember, that's 101, 102, 105, 106 AD, something like that.'

'Apparently, there are symbols from Calgacus's time. Caledonian symbols hiding in the relief,' said Susan.

'Well, it's a column and there's a relief that winds all the way around it.'

'Well, according to Hamish, the relief has symbols within it. Symbols put there very early on. Prisoners brought over. Prisoners who were held in the Basilica Julia. Kept and tortured. Some of them managed to escape and infiltrate society. They've been here for years.'

'Secret societies are not that uncommon,' said Matteo. 'I could believe that. So what? They meet every so often; they—'

'No,' said Susan. 'He said that the secret society is still operating. But he's trying to work out their malevolent intent. Hang on a minute,' she said.

Susan left Matteo hanging on her words while she read ahead. After five minutes, he tapped her foot.

'Okay, okay. Listen. He made connections with some of them. Says that when he first arrived, and he started tracing Calgacus, he found the symbols. Then he found stories hidden away, symbology in various items at the Capitoline Museums. He was deeply intrigued. One of his big issues was he wanted to get to the Vatican Secret Archives, but he didn't know how to get in. He believed the Vatican was aware of this cult of Calgacus.'

'Well, he's going to have to do better than that,' said Matteo. 'I'm not walking in to my boss telling him I need to see the Papal Father to have a discussion about some Caledonian chieftain the Romans killed some time ago.'

'Well, we both can agree on that,' said Susan. 'But in terms of where he went, he doesn't say he got into the Vatican Secret Archives. He did get documentation, however. Although he notes he didn't get to keep it or photograph it, it showed this cult was real, and the lineage of many of the surrounding people was real.'

'Does he give names?'

'Not here.'

'Well, I don't know where we go then,' said Matteo. 'He's not got evidence, so to speak. Supposition, and it's—'

'His evidence is not here. It's not recorded,' said Susan. 'It's not been photographed. He said he's seen it. We'd have to go into the Vatican Secret Archive to find it—'

'They're not letting you in for that,' said Matteo. 'Well, we'd have to have a very good reason to be in there. This is a book that doesn't have evidence, yet pertains to the archive being at the centre of something. There are rumours galore about that archive and what's in it.'

'I can get that,' said Susan. 'I'm not here to cause a diplomatic incident.'

'So what's the plan of action then?' asked Matteo.

'Well, what we know from the book is he went to the Basilica Julia and the Capitoline Museums. Maybe we go there, check their CCTV, find out if anybody spoke to him. See if we can find anybody connected with him.'

'Sounds like a good idea,' said Matteo. He put his hand down momentarily on Susan's thigh. And then he stopped himself.

'I was just trying to push myself up. Sorry.'

'It's fine.' And it really was fine with Susan. The touch was exciting, yes, but she wasn't sad that it had now discontinued. She was most happy about how she felt about her leg, about the fact that somebody went near it and she didn't pull away.

'Why don't you get some sleep tonight and in the morning, we can see the museums and the Basilica Julia?'

'Why not go tonight?'

'Why?' asked Matteo.

'We haven't got that long. From the sound of it, your boss is going to kick us off this case quickly. We need to make the most of our time.'

'Well, I'm going to organise it. It'll be after hours. I'll need somebody to help us get in. It might take me a while and I also want to go home and change. I think if we go in later, we should go in much later, when the place is truly quiet.'

'That's fine,' said Susan.

'What are you going to do?' asked Matteo.

'I'm going to relax here for an hour or two. Then come get me.'

'Very good,' said Matteo, smiling at her. He looked like he was about to say something, but then he didn't. She didn't force the issue. She didn't want to know how he felt; if he was just being kind, or if he actually felt anything more than that. If he was in Italy, far away, he was a non-starter.

Instead, she let him walk out and leave her alone by the poolside. She reached down, pulled on her white t-shirt, pulling it off and leaving it beside her. Susan lay back on the recliner in her bikini. She had been like this so many times on holiday. Happy to lie there. Happy to let the world see her, almost proud in her body, and now she almost felt that way

CHAPTER 06

again, despite how her leg was. She smiled. This trip had been good for her, very good for her.

Chapter 07

Susan had her eyes closed when she heard the vibration of her phone. She opened them quickly, still lying at the poolside, even though it was getting late. The wind was cooler now, but not unpleasant, just cooler, not cold. Matteo might have been freezing, might even have shivered, but not Susan. She was well used to the winters back in the Highlands. This was delightful. She grabbed the phone though, pressing the button, and she saw it was Macleod on the other end.

'How goes it?' he asked.

'Okay,' she said. 'I'm assisting them.'

'I haven't interrupted you, have I?' asked Macleod.

'Of course not, Seoras,' said Susan. 'You're always welcome to call.'

'It wasn't a social call, it is an official update I'm looking for,' said Macleod.

'Getting on with the case, and it seems our Scottish friend had been working on uncovering some sort of ancient society. All the way back to Calgacus.'

'Calgacus,' said Macleod. 'It's not ringing a bell.'

'You'd have to be a bit of a history buff. He was a Caledonian leader back in the day. Fought against the Romans, ultimately defeated, but held up as a bit of a hero.'

'Caledonia? You mean Scotland?'

'No, Seoras, Caledonia, as was the ancient land. Not quite the same as today's Scotland.'

'I'm not a history buff,' said Macleod, 'so I'll take your word for it. But it's all going okay.'

'I'm contributing. Getting about okay. Helping out.'

'Is it an open and shut case, though? Are they just doing due diligence? What's your take?' asked Macleod.

'There might be something in this,' Susan said. 'Possible he was murdered, but too early to say.'

'Well, speculate then,' said Macleod.

'My money would be on something dodgy going on, but I need some more evidence to get anybody else to go along with that. Their Chief Inspector, as such, he's seeing it as an open and shut case. Just get on with it. Believes he died of natural causes, or rather from a trip or a fall. Quick brush under the carpet.'

'Need any assistance?' asked Macleod. 'If you think something's afoot—'

'Seoras, it could well be a wild goose chase, to be honest. They're probably right; it is an old story. Ferguson probably did just fall over or jump. He was a genealogist, into all that history stuff. He talks of secret societies and things. It's one of those moments when you can see conspiracy in everything.'

'Well, keep me updated,' said Macleod. 'If any further assistance is required, it's not a problem.'

'What, you would send Perry out?'

'Come out myself,' said Macleod.

'Long way for you to come just for that.'

'To do what?' said Macleod. 'To come out and lie by a pool

in a sun lounger?'

There's a silence at Cunningham's end of the phone. And then she realised and laughed.

'I'm not having a go at you,' said Macleod. 'I can't hear the traffic, I can't hear anything. I can usually tell if I'm in a busy city, so I'm thinking you might be beside the pool. Time of night it is, you should be off work, anyway. As should I. I'm going home. Just keep me updated.'

Susan agreed she would and then made for her room to get changed. Putting on some light trousers and a top, she waited for another twenty minutes before Matteo sent her a text asking to meet her at the ground floor of the hotel.

From there, they made their way to the Capitoline Museums. The place was quiet and yet the building was fascinating, grandiose, with all the artefacts laid out. Yet Susan thought it lost a bit of its life without people. Exhibits were meant to be exhibited, to be looked at. Not to sit simply in what now looked like a rather well-laid-out, but basic storeroom.

Matteo found the man he had contacted earlier and introduced him to Susan. He instantly offered her a seat, spotting she had a crutch. Susan shook her head, answering back politely in Italian, when he'd offered his suggestion in English. After that, she let Matteo take the conversation.

The guy had remembered Hamish, and how he was looking at various objects for days on end. The curator had taken him round, pointing out these objects, but he couldn't see anything particularly fascinating. When Matteo mentioned Calgacus and history possibly being interwoven into some of the objects, the curator just laughed.

'Yes, he said that about them.'

'What did he talk about with you,' asked Matteo, 'when he

came to ask about objects?'

'He was interested in stories he'd heard about Caledonian prisoners in the Basilica Julia. I don't think those stories are real; they're rumours,' said the man.

'What sort of rumours? Do they have a bit of fact in them, or—'

'Long, long story. Nothing still existing to corroborate and so the truth is unproven. True legend.'

'So, nothing you would take seriously. Lost material.'

'Nothing I could take seriously as a historian. Nothing to back them up. However, there's nothing to say they weren't true either. Just, well, one thing lost to history possibly or something that never happened at all.'

'Was there anything else about the Scottish man that struck you?' asked Matteo.

'Well, his going to the baths one night.'

'The baths?'

'The baths of Diocletian.'

'I'm sorry, it's been so long since my school history days. Why's that strange?'

'They were built long after Calgacus's time,' said the curator, 'which is why I was a bit perplexed when he mentioned it. Yet they were the main social area of Rome. Deals were done. Business was talked. The baths were a social place as much as anything. A club you went to.'

'But why was the Scottish man going to the baths?' asked Susan.

'He said there was a function there,' said the curator. 'I don't know of any function that was there. It certainly wasn't advertised.'

'And he was asking you about them?' said Matteo.

'As much as he asked about everything else. He seemed like a man who was a sponge taking everything in, but he seemed to ingest everything—wasn't very discerning.'

'Did you feel there was anything in what he was saying?' asked Matteo.

'Typical tourist. They want to believe in the fantastic and the romantic, don't they? I'm a historian. I have to search for fact, as they say, not for fantasy, not for what I wish it to be.'

Matteo shook his hand, as did Susan, and the pair left.

'Shall we go to the baths?' asked Susan.

'Good idea. I don't know if anybody will be there. There might be some security on,' said Matteo.

'We could check for any functions this season. And if there was, maybe there'll be CCTV.'

'It's a good idea,' said Matteo. 'I need to call ahead to them.'

At the baths, Matteo found a security guard. He asked to talk that night about the various functions the Baths had put on. But instead the guard offered to let them talk to someone the next day who might know better.

'We might do that,' said Matteo, 'but I'd like the CCTV footage from the time.'

'I could give you it tomorrow.'

'We could look tonight,' said Susan. 'I'm not doing anything.'

Matteo smiled. He disappeared off with the security guard before coming back with several data sticks.

'There's quite a lot of footage to watch here. Are you sure you want to do this?'

'Absolutely,' said Susan.

'You always this dogged?' asked Matteo.

'I've been taught to be dogged by the boss,' said Susan. 'And also, I don't have long here, so the more I can get done, the

CHAPTER 07

more satisfied I'll be that we came to the right conclusion.'

'Just don't wear yourself out,' insisted Matteo.

Susan wondered why he was so keen to get down to the investigation as well. If they'd been at home, the first thing they would have done was save this video for the morning. Susan was only going at this because she didn't have long. Matteo did though. He would be here for a while. And even if his boss had said to wrap it up, he'd still be able to wrangle a bit of investigating afterwards. That's what Susan would have done.

Back at the station, Susan realised just how much quieter it was at the Inverness station. Things got quieter through the night. But this was Rome. And so while the station seemed quieter, the number of people about was still high. Matteo took Susan off to an enclosed room with banks of computers and sat down there, ready to watch the CCTV footage.

The footage ran long into the night until Matteo spotted a meeting. It wasn't difficult. The time frame wasn't too accurate, but once he knew the date and the time, the collated CCTV footage told a different story. There had been a gathering. A significant one.

'Look at that,' said Matteo. 'Do you notice something?'

'I notice many people gathering.'

'No. Something more than that. That man there, for instance—he's a priest.'

Susan looked at him. He was wearing what looked like corduroy trousers, a jumper. There was no sign he was a priest, though, as far as she could see.

'Doesn't look like a priest.'

'No, he's a priest out of his holy garment,' said Matteo.

'How can you tell?' asked Susan.

'Because I know him. Sorry,' said Matteo. 'That was unfair, wasn't it? There are several well-known people here, on what looks like a quiet function.'

'You say well-known people. How well-known?'

'Well, not pop-star fame,' said Matteo. 'But there are some minor politicians. There are people from the church. There's certain businesspeople there. A rather strange collection for what looks like a normally quiet function. It's not been advertised, it's not gone on the calendar, and they're all swarming in and not queuing to go in. It looks unorganised in some ways. Either that or everybody just knows what to do.'

'You mean like a group that's done it before,' said Susan.

'Exactly,' said Matteo. 'Exactly.' He pulled out a pad of paper and wrote the names of all the people he recognised. 'See this group of people here?'

'What about them?'

'Well, there's no criminal underworld there, but there's a significant slice of society, one that could certainly influence. One that could pull a few strings if they got together.'

'So, what are they all there for?' asked Susan.

'Well,' said Matteo. 'I find it unusual they're together for a start. So, there must be something connecting them.'

'Hamish said there was a cult of Calgacus.'

'Most of these people are Italian. In fact, they're nearly all Italian,' said Matteo.

'But Calgacus was about historical context. About lineage. After all, Hamish was a genealogist. That's why he's got on to this. Maybe these people are not so Roman as they appear. You should read what Hamish Ferguson wrote.'

'Are you sure we're not clutching at straws here? That's how you put it, isn't it, in English?'

CHAPTER 07

'It is indeed. Maybe we should take a visit in the morning,' said Susan, looking at her watch. 'It is half-past three.'

'Let's get you back to your room and to bed,' said Matteo. 'I'll sort a visit to the Baths. We'll go there early, find out what's going on. See what this is, whether it's just some innocent gathering or whether it's this cult that our man is talking about.'

Susan swung down off the chair and grabbed her crutch. She was tired, exhausted. But she was also extremely happy.

Chapter 08

Susan Cunningham was feeling lively despite the lack of sleep. She'd only grabbed maybe three hours back at the hotel. She wasn't sure if Matteo had any more, but they both were invigorated as they left her hotel and got into his car. Racing across Rome, navigating the busy streets into what seemed like chaotic traffic to Susan, the pair of them didn't complain once. Susan thought they made a good team. She was happy that Matteo was supporting her and following almost every comment of hers.

'The boss called last night,' said Susan.

'What's he like?' asked Matteo.

'I think you'd like him, although he takes a bit of a while to get used to. He's quite dour, not the most lively of persons, but he's brilliant. He sees things in people; sees things before a lot of other people do. Quite often with him, he knows who's done it before he's actually got all the evidence. Out of fairness to him, he's quite considerate. That's why I'm out here.'

Matteo smiled for a moment but gave a quizzical look. 'You're out here because he's very kind? He sent someone with, no offence intended, half a leg to help conduct an investigation.'

'He knew I needed time away, that I needed to sort myself.

So that's why I'm here.'

'And I thought you were here because of your abilities,' said Matteo.

'Well, that too,' said Susan. 'He wouldn't send a dummy out. He knows I can handle this.'

'I hope so,' said Matteo, suddenly looking absentmindedly out of the window.

What sort of comment was that? A strange one. 'I don't think we'll find anything at the Baths,' speculated Susan.

'Well, we'll soon find out,' said Matteo. 'It's just around the corner.'

The Baths of Diocletian were impressive, to say the least. There was the usual tourist bumph around them, explaining what it was, why it was here. But the Baths themselves were magnificent, despite their age. The grey stonework still resonated to Susan, and she could see all the men wrapped in their towels discussing this and that as they sat among the baths.

It was the same nowadays though, wasn't it? All going to the health clubs, coffee, Jacuzzis, or on the squash court. There was always some sort of leisure around business, something that drove people to communicate together, open up more than a conference room ever did.

Maybe Macleod should start a similar scheme. She could talk to him in the squash court. Susan thought about Macleod playing squash. She laughed a little.

'What's that for?' asked Matteo.

'Just an image I've got in my head. Don't worry, it's not of you.'

'I hope not,' said Matteo. 'I've been nice to you.'

'Yes, you have,' said Susan. 'You've been incredibly kind.

Thank you. Some people would just get fed up. Your boss didn't look very impressed when I hobbled in.'

'Didn't take the time to get to know you. If somebody sends someone who's struggling to an international investigation, he must think very highly of them. That he thinks you can cope with that, on top of other things.'

'That's one way of looking at it,' said Susan. 'I know other people who would just get rid of me. Have me out of their hair for a while.'

'You must be special to them back in Scotland.'

Matteo disappeared, looking for a contact, and came back with a caretaker who was looking quite perturbed.

'Meeting here,' she said. 'At that time of night, late, there would be nobody here.'

'Do you not know about this meeting?' asked Susan.

'Clearly not,' the caretaker said. 'There can't have been a meeting,' she continued, shaking her head in disbelief.

Taking out his phone, Matteo played a brief clip of the meeting in progress, taken from the CCTV.

'There was nothing mentioned about that. And that's not fair,' said the woman.

'Not fair?' said Susan, in her best Italian.

'No, it is not fair, because that would require overtime. And I didn't get any.'

The woman grabbed Matteo's phone and looked at it again. When she handed it back, she looked at him quizzically. 'Do you know which day that was?'

'Yes,' said Matteo, showing what day it was to her.

'Right,' she said. 'It strikes me I discovered something similar, something unusual that I stumbled upon. I think the day is the same,' she said. 'Come with me.'

CHAPTER 08

Matteo and Susan were led by the woman into the rear of the baths. The room held the lockers for the staff, but she made a direct line for one of them. Opening it, the woman reached inside. There were shoes, but also a small shelf with various other items. It looked like any locker, one owned by someone who'd been in a place for a long time. There was rubbish sitting on a shelf that you never have quite been bothered to clear out.'

'There's a little note here,' she said. 'A brief note that I couldn't make out.'

'I don't understand,' said Matteo.

'I didn't get the importance of it,' she said.

'Still not understanding you,' said Matteo. 'What do you mean?'

The woman reached inside the locker, and she took out what looked like a scrumped-up note. She unwrapped it, and then she handed it to Matteo, saying, 'You see, the place was spotless that morning. When we go away at night, the cleaners come in, and they do an okay job, but this one was spotless. This looked like everything had been cleaned out. But that's not common. That's a deep clean. We have to be careful how we clean here. Certain parts of it, you don't want to ruin the historical aspects.'

Susan could appreciate that. But the level of annoyance on the woman's face was rising. 'We don't come in and clean like that. It was that day, the one of your gathering. I mentioned it, but nobody took me up on it.'

'But what is this?' asked Matteo, looking at the scrumped-up piece of paper.

'This' said the woman, unravelling it and placing it down in front of them, 'is a location and a time. It seems strange to me. It was just lying there, so I kept it. I was intending to see if anybody knew about it, but I forgot about it, and it's been sitting on that shelf in my locker ever since. Nobody else knows about it except me.'

'What do you think it is?' asked Matteo.

'How would I know?' said the woman. 'It's a location, and it's just a street, an ordinary street in the poor areas. I visited it during the day at one point, but I couldn't see anything. And I was keeping it until the date and time had gone. But the date is today.'

'Great.' Susan stared at the paper. The date and day was today. The time was later on this evening. 'So, nobody else knows about this?'

'No,' said the woman.

'And nobody's come looking for it?'

'No one. Nobody's asked. Nobody's even come with an excuse, even if they'd haven't asked about it directly, to ask about other things.'

'Well, then. Thank you for that,' said Matteo. 'It might be nothing, of course. It might be somebody's arrangement for a dinner. Maybe somebody's getting picked up from there.'

The woman didn't look impressed with that response. With a scowl towards Matteo, she showed Susan and him out to the primary thoroughfares of the Baths. It was getting busy now, tourists arriving, and Matteo and Susan took their leave. They drove to a small cafe where they sat outside in the sun with two cups of espresso.

'How do you think this is going?' asked Matteo,

'What do you mean?' asked Susan.

'How do you think it's going?'

'There's been plenty of questions around Ferguson's movements, haven't there?' she said.

'I think so, but my boss seems to think this is an accident.'

'But does he know about what we're discovering? He didn't know about the book. He didn't—'

'He knows now, and he's still saying it's an open and shut case. He thinks that Hamish Ferguson is a madman, or a lunatic, chasing up dead people and historic elements.'

'Do you think that?' asked Susan.

'No. Having seen the footage of those people meeting, I want to know why they were there. Those people don't meet like that for no reason. It wasn't advertised. It wasn't even advertised on the non-public networks, so to speak.

'Certain events in Rome are only for the elite. You don't advertise those. Well, not in that way. They get advertised in a different way. And certain people would always receive an invitation for them. They didn't receive an invitation for that. Hamish Ferguson's talking about a cult. Have you any experience of cults?'

Susan nearly rolled her eyes. Did she have any experience of cults? Her own boss nearly got killed by a cult. 'Well, we've had a few instances back home.'

'The problem is,' said Matteo, 'is we need to link these people back to Calgacus. If we do that, then there's a very positive link. If we don't, then there's a modest link. Was Hamish Ferguson just hopping on to any conspiracy theory he could find? Or was this just a group who were fairly secret and he joined them, got involved with them, even though they were nothing to do with what he was looking at?'

'Yes,' said Susan. 'Hard to say at the moment.'

'But we've got lucky,' said Matteo, 'haven't we?'

'It is lucky. Are you thinking we're too lucky?' asked Susan.

'I don't know. Could it be some sort of set-up?'

'But why set-up us at all? When your boss is thinking it's a damp squib, what does sending us to them mean? It's better to just let us wander round in the dark and not get anywhere.'

'That's exactly what I think,' said Matteo, 'and that's why I think it's genuine. But tonight, we need to go on stakeout. I think we pay a visit tonight, but we do it discreetly.'

'About that,' said Susan, 'how does a person like myself go about being discreet? I'll have a crutch with me. I'll have a half a leg missing. They're going to go, "Oh look, there's that British police officer, the one with half a leg missing. What's she doing here?"'

'Give yourself some credit,' said Matteo. 'You can do this.'

Susan said, 'I'll go tonight with one crutch, not the two. I need to get used to that, anyway.'

'You don't need to come at all if you don't want to,' said Matteo. 'This could be tricky, depending on who's there. If it comes to talking to people, let me do it. I know who they are. I know how to approach them. What we don't need is people thinking that you Brits are taking over.'

'Did I give that impression?' Susan laughed.

'Not at all.'

'Let me take it to your inspector then; tell him what we're doing.'

'No,' said Matteo, quite abruptly, 'we don't need to tell him what we're doing.'

'Why?' asked Susan. 'I would always run past what I'm doing with my DCI, with Macleod. It's just a courtesy.'

'Maybe I need to talk to you about something,' said Matteo. 'I wasn't going to. I didn't want to reel you in too far.'

'What?' asked Susan. Matteo looked around him. Then he

crouched down in his seat again. 'Tell me,' said Susan. 'What's the worst it can be?'

'Sometimes I think, my inspector, Inspector Ricci, is not quite what he appears to be. I think he may work for other people. Or at least be taking slush money from them. That's how you describe it, isn't it?

'We have many groups that are involved in organised crime in Italy. You've got the Mafia Capitale, exposed in 2014, but it's still there. The Camorra, who came up from Naples to make the operations here. Then 'Ndrangheta, a Calabrian organised crime group. The Costa Nostra, which you probably know about. The Sacro Corona, originally from Puglia. Some from outside of this country.

'I've believed my inspector has, at times, compromised himself. I don't think he's out and out against law and order, but he chooses to make something for himself. Obviously, I can't say any of this to anyone, can I?'

'Of course not. You'll lose your job.'

'Well, in that case, we'll go and we'll investigate the Baths.'

'Yes, but we'll do it discreetly. Or discreetly as I can. And then, if we've got proper evidence, we'll take it in. It might be easier to bring in the weight of the UK government to say that they need to get an answer in this. Make Hamish Ferguson out to be more than just some random genealogist. I could probably do that.'

'I think what we need to do is form some sort of plan about how we do our visit tonight. Maybe I'll contact my boss or higher up,' said Matteo. 'Trouble is that I don't know how far this stretches, and I want nothing to compromise what's going on in this investigation. I guess it'll have to be just between you and me. Okay?'

'Okay,' said Susan. 'If that's what you insist.'

'I do,' said Matteo, before offering Susan another espresso. 'We'll be going there this evening to pay a visit.'

Susan didn't like what Matteo was suggesting. She'd know evidence of Ricci's wrongdoing, so she'd have to trust Matteo. Was this why Ricci was pushing the case to a close? If they could get twenty-four hours, maybe forty-eight at the most. And then, everything would go to at least Macleod, if no one else.

Chapter 09

'So, what are you saying?' asked Macleod. He lifted his eyes to look over at the other person in the room. Jane, his partner, was sitting on a seat at the far wall. She had a cup of coffee beside her and was sipping on it gently. Her legs were crossed over, however, a sure sign that she wanted to get on her way.

She didn't sit down with her legs crossed. They were always simply placed side by side. But when she got agitated and wanted to get on the move, she would cross them, and then they would uncross and cross again.

There you go, thought Macleod, watching her. He just needed to get Clarissa off the phone. Maybe he had wound her up too much. He'd taken Hope for breakfast. Well-deserved as well, after her rescue antics with the bomber. But Clarissa had seen it as an affront. She was petulant when you got down to it. There was that side to her, a side that came hand-in-hand with that dogged determination, that run-around terrier that she was.

Rottweiler, that was what they called her. She was his Rottweiler. Well, she would have to develop into more than that. She was a DI now, not a sergeant. Not there simply to do his bidding, but there to work out what to do and how to do it. And then tell him what she was doing. Not wait for instruction.

Macleod stifled a yawn. She seemed to be doing okay. She was just in that phase when it took time to dig things up. But her tone was almost petulant. She was angry with him, as if she needed to be told that she'd done well. Macleod didn't give out badges.

He was now a DCI. He expected his people to have taken that on board. Yes, sometimes when the younger uniform officers were working with you, you picked them up; you built them because they were still wondering if they were in the right role. Clarissa had chosen hers. There was no reason for her to be led like a puppy. She needed to look to her team now.

Her team—Emmett Grump had joined them. *A funny little man*, Macleod thought. *Clever. Brilliant. He'd be a struggle for her. He didn't like fashion. Wasn't really into the art scene. And was incredibly quiet. But Patterson was good for her. Eric Patterson, whose life she'd saved. And he'd now,* Macleod saw, *become her second.*

'I'm going to have to go,' said Macleod. 'Jane's in here. We're having lunch.'

'Oh, aye. Is there any woman you don't take out for a meal other than me?'

'No,' said Macleod. And he could hear the anger down the phone. 'We'll speak later,' he said. He put the phone down.

'You stop winding her up,' said Jane.

'What do you mean?' asked Macleod, standing up. He turned for a moment to look out his window.

'You know fine well what I mean, Seoras. You wouldn't treat Hope like that.'

'I don't have to treat Hope like that. It's not the way Hope behaves. Clarissa's . . . she's something else. Good copper, though,' said Macleod. 'If you can point her in the right direction.'

'She doesn't have it easy. You know that, don't you?'

'None of us have it easy, Jane. She's an older woman. Yet she dresses like, well, something from some insane Scottish parody,' said Macleod suddenly.

'You've been holding that one in,' said Jane.

'Yes,' said Macleod. 'And the little green car and all the rest of it. She's good at what she does. I wouldn't have asked her to head up that team if I didn't think so. I don't just . . .'

'You're talking to me,' said Jane. 'I know you don't just do things for ease. You do them because you think you're right about them. And you probably are right with her. Be a little easier on her.'

'She needs to get by on her own. She needs to take the lead.'

'Well, sometimes it takes people time, doesn't it?'

'Are we going for lunch,' said Macleod, 'or am I going to be receiving all this advice for the rest of the afternoon?'

'I'm the one waiting for you. I have been ready for a while.'

'Can tell,' he said. 'You're crossing your legs again.'

Jane looked at him. 'I have told you, none of the detective stuff with me, okay? What you had to do there was to stay quiet and just say, "Let's go."'

'Then let's go,' said Macleod. He walked over to the door of his office, grabbed his coat, and put it over his arm. He took his hat and popped it on his head.

'You know what, Seoras Macleod? You almost look presentable.'

Macleod raised his eyebrows. 'I think you'll find I'm one of the most . . .'

'Get out,' said Jane. She smacked him on the backside. He gave a little jump, then opened the door for her. Everyone saw Macleod as a very staid and quiet man. A serious man. But Jane brought something alive in him. They were almost playful together. None of that came from him, but he loved it. She was his time away from all the darkness that he saw in the job. She kept him on a level. Kept him as a man who was still human, and not destroyed by the darkness he saw.

'So what's Clarissa bugging you about now?'

'The breakfast I took Hope for,' said Macleod. 'I mean, it was a nice breakfast and that. But she's going on and on about it, how she didn't get one.'

'Well, I hope my lunch is at least as expensive.'

'Of course not,' said Macleod. 'Hope's breakfast was on expenses.' Jane turned round and punched him on the arm.

As he drove the car to the restaurant for lunch, Macleod stared out of the window. Every now and again, he seemed to drift away from the road in front of him, losing focus.

'What's up?' asked Jane.

'Why should something be up?' said Macleod.

'Seoras. Quit it. Okay. This is me. What's up?'

'Susan Cunningham went over to Italy to help them out with the death of a British tourist. I haven't heard from her in over thirty-six hours. She was doing well with it. It's just that . . .'

'What?'

'She said she was probably coming back soon. She said the case was a non-starter, except it wasn't. She said there might be something in it, and I haven't heard from her.'

'Was she meant to check in?'

'There's no specific timeframe, but I'm the boss. You check

CHAPTER 09

in with me. Even Clarissa checks in with me.'

'Why don't you ring her?'

'She lost her leg,' said Macleod. 'I was trying to give her some space, and it seemed to be working. She'd met an officer over there. They were getting on well. She was enjoying herself while working. I don't want to intrude.'

'You're the boss, you just told me. DCI. You don't intrude. You just check up.'

'That sounds worse,' said Macleod. 'Besides, I contacted Inspector Ricci. He's a strange one. Maybe his English and my Italian aren't the best. But he said that he thought Susan was enjoying herself. He said the case was a non-starter.'

'And?'

'Something's bugging me,' said Macleod. 'Non-starter. Okay. I can get the case could be a non-starter. But Susan was being thorough. Making sure it was. And now I haven't heard from her.'

Macleod pulled the car into the car park. 'Anyway, that's for when I get back to the office. This is your time with me, and this is lunch.'

'You're worried, aren't you?'

'Yes,' Macleod. 'But I don't really much need to be.'

'And that's worrying you even more.'

'It's one of those detective things you learn. Something's not right in the blood, making you agitated. Something's banging away in the back of your head.'

'Have some lunch; maybe it'll come to you.'

'Maybe it will,' Macleod said. He stepped out of the car and took Jane's arm as they entered the restaurant.

Macleod was finishing his coffee and the small piece of cheesecake that was left on his plate. Jane was smiling. She liked restaurants, enjoyed eating. She liked dating with him, for Jane wasn't a difficult woman. All she wanted was a bit of your time and she to be in your company.

He'd seen enough relationships in his working life to know that things could go badly wrong and he was grateful for what they had. He cast a surreptitious look at his watch. Maybe he'd get away with another fifteen minutes and then he'd have to get back. There was that meeting this afternoon. He hated these meetings. Manpower, resources, budgets. Hated them all.

Macleod's phone vibrated. He reached for it straight away, but gave an 'excuse me' to June. She told him she was never bothered by the fact he had to be contacted at the times they were together. But she said a polite 'excuse me' let her know he was thinking of her first. He thought that was fair enough.

Macleod looked at the phone. It was a text message, asking for a leave of absence, for a week to recuperate in the Mediterranean sun. While formally written, it came from Susan Cunningham's phone.

'What's up?' asked Jane. Clearly, the issue was written across his face as a problem.

'It's from Susan. Says she wants a leave of absence for a week. Stay out in the sun. Says the case is a non-starter.'

'Does it say anything else?' asked Jane.

'Says she has to get her head in order before coming back.'

'That sounds fair enough.'

'The idea of it, yes,' said Macleod. 'But not how it's been done. She's asking for a week of absence. And she doesn't ask for a week of absence from me. That's Hope's to give, not mine. She's out working for me with a case, so she should contact me to say that the case is wound up, and then go to Hope to ask to stay out.'

Macleod was about to look further into the text when his phone vibrated again. He answered the call that was coming through. 'Hello, DCI Macleod?'

'Yes, this is Macleod.'

'Inspector Ricci again, from Rome. I've just had my superintendent ask for a week's leave. Matteo, I think, is looking to help your Susan Cunningham. He's talked about them being off on a road trip.'

'A road trip?' said Macleod. 'What's happening with the case?'

'It's a dead end. The man fell. I'm sorry to have wasted her time in bringing her out here, but it seems to have done her good. It can't have been easy for a woman to lose a leg like that.'

'No, it wasn't,' said Macleod, almost absentmindedly. He was about to ask whether they were sure that the man had fallen, and that there was no foul play involved. But if somebody did that to him after he had stated it, he would have seen it as being highly disrespectful.

'Well, she'll be okay from this end,' said Macleod. 'Thank you for contacting me.'

'Maybe one day we'll meet in person,' said Ricci. 'She's a credit to your force. I hope to see you one day,' he closed down the phone call. Jane was watching him, but Macleod stood up and waved over at the waitress, indicating he wanted the bill.

'What's up, Seoras?'

'That was the inspector from Italy. Says Susan's gone on a road trip with one of his people for the week. Says the case is all closed down.'

'You don't believe him?'

'I'm not happy,' said Macleod. 'Something's wrong. Off. Sorry, I need to get back to the office.'

'It's fine,' said Jane. 'I'll grab the bill,' she said. 'You get back to the office.'

'It's my treat.'

'It's a joint credit card,' said Jane. 'It's not about treats anymore, it's about us.' She stood up and walked round to him, kissing him on the cheek. 'Go find out what's going on and let me know what you're doing,' said Jane.

'Will do. Sorry,' he said. 'One day, we'll finish the meal properly.'

'You make it sound like this happens all the time.'

'Happens more often than I would want it to,' he said. Putting his arms around her, he hugged her and kissed her, and then tore off out of the restaurant. Something was wrong.

It was only fifteen minutes later, when Macleod, still dressed in his coat with his hat, erupted through the door of Hope McGrath's office. She was on the phone, but she quickly put it down as he came in.

'Sorry,' he said.

'Are you okay?' asked Hope. 'Not like you to barge in.'

'No,' he said. 'Not okay.' He reached back and closed the door behind him. 'Have you heard from Susan?'

'But she's working for you. I'm not expecting to hear from her.'

'She's apparently asking for a leave of absence. A text message came through for me.'

'She texted you for a leave of absence? I thought that was my responsibility.'

'It is. And she knows that,' said Macleod. 'She also knows that she's working for me at the moment out there, not you.

Therefore, if the case is a non-starter, she should be telling me that. I had a phone call from Inspector Ricci out there saying that was the case. Saying that she'd disappeared off in a car with one of his people. And they were going for a week in the sun.'

'She could do with a week in the sun,' said Hope.

'I don't doubt that,' said Macleod. 'But there is no way she would ask for it like this."

Susan's not disrespectful in that way,' said Hope. 'Strange.'

Hope suddenly reached round to her back pocket, pulling a phone out of her jeans. 'Seoras,' she said. 'You better look at this.' She held up the phone in front of Macleod, and he peered at the screen. The words, 'help, over my head, hunting me,' were on the phone.

'Who's that from?' asked Macleod. He felt he knew the answer.

'That's from Susan,' said Hope, 'except that's not her police sim card. Not the one she uses normally. That's her private and personal one.'

'I don't have that number,' said Macleod.

'No, you don't. Only I do in this office. Her police phone says she's off on holiday. Her private one says she's being hunted,' said Macleod. 'Get Ross onto that phone now. Find out where that message came from.' He went to turn.

'What are you going to do?' asked Hope.

'She's on foreign soil. She's away. I've got an inspector who's touting the story that she's gone off with someone else. I'm off to see Jim. And work out what on earth to do about this.'

Chapter 10

The ACC walked into Hope's office and sat down in a chair by her desk. Hope gave him a polite smile and watched as Ross produced the coffee, placing it in front of the area commander. Jim had his run-ins with Hope with Macleod, but he was the direct boss, even though the last time they'd had a serious meeting, Hope had nearly chewed the face off him. But that was because the man had got it wrong, heavily wrong, and Hope had gone against him in order to save people's lives. She hoped they would now be on a more level playing field, that he would listen more willingly.'

'Macleod said this was urgent.'

'Very,' said Hope, 'but I'll let him explain it. It's a closed office job, though.'

Hope reached forward and took a sip of her coffee. 'That'll be all, Ross,' said Hope. 'Thank you for that.'

'The DCI's coffee's just out here. I'll intercept him when he comes in.'

'Just bring it in now,' said Hope. 'Once we go into conference, I don't want anyone coming through that door, please, Sergeant.'

She rarely used the word sergeant with Ross. It was Alan.

CHAPTER 10

Or it was Ross. But she wanted him to understand that this would be formal, very formal and very private, with no hint of annoyance.

Ross walked back out of the office before bringing in Macleod's coffee and placing it on the table in front of the empty chair.

It was five minutes later when Macleod broke the awkward silence in the office, closing the door behind him.

'Seoras, what's going on?'

'Thanks for coming down, Jim. I take it Hope hasn't briefed you then yet?'

'I thought it should come from you. You're the one in the middle of it,' said Hope. 'I have got no written facts to go through. Best if you describe everything.'

Macleod nodded and took a sip of the coffee that had been left by Ross. He then smiled at Jim. 'I think I may have to go undercover to Italy.'

Jim nearly spat his own coffee out. 'What?'

'Listen to this.' Macleod ran Jim through what had happened, detailing the case up to that point. And then Susan's supposed text.

'So, at the moment you think what?' asked Jim.

'I think she's on the run. I think she's come across something in the case. Somebody's gone off with her.'

'Are they involved in it too? Are they . . . being hunted?'

As I understand it, Matteo was the superintendent working with Susan. They must have stumbled across something together that other people don't want to know. Ricci, the inspector, called me. He gave the line of what Susan was doing—taking time off along with Matteo. So the whole official line is that she's asking for some leave and the case is a non-starter. And then we get this.'

Hope placed her phone in front of Jim. 'That came to me. The number is Susan Cunningham's private number. Her private SIM card. Nobody else in the office has that number. We all use a police phone. Except me. She gave it to me.'

'Are you sure that this came from her?'

'Ross says that it's her number, but it was used on a public computer in a library in Rome.'

'Help, over my head, hunting me,' said Macleod. 'We need to act quickly. I'm afraid for her.'

'We're on foreign soil,' said Jim. 'Look, we should do this formally. We should ask properly what's going on with . . .'

'No! We shouldn't,' said Macleod. 'At least not just yet. We need to look at this differently. If Ricci's involved, if certain figures in the police force are involved, she may have found something there in the library. Susan's a good copper. She's also somebody who wouldn't be afraid to investigate the authorities doing something wrong.'

'What's she doing out there, anyway? I thought she'd lost half a leg,' said Jim.

'She hasn't lost her brain,' said Macleod. 'She'll get over the leg, or rather, she'll learn to live without it. Best thing for her was to get out somewhere else. Here, everybody was pitying her. Here she had Perry looking after her. She needed some space on her own, to find her own feet, so to speak,' said Macleod.

'I'm with Seoras on this one,' said Hope. 'I think we need to get out there. I think I should go.'

'No,' said Macleod. 'I got her into it. I should be the one to sort it.'

'When did that ever become the reason we send anyone

CHAPTER 10

anywhere?' said Jim.

'We're not just talking about being deployed. We're talking about going undercover. We're talking about possibly having to get left on a hanger if you get caught out there,' said Macleod. 'Career ending.'

'Are you asking to just go?' said Jim.

'Yes,' said Macleod.

'You're in your sixties. Come off it,' said Hope. 'You're not fit enough to run around out there.'

'Hope,' said Macleod. 'You're six feet tall, you've got bright red hair, and you are the face of this force during the public consultations, during the media sessions. Your face is well known too. My face is well known to anybody around Inverness.

'I am not well known in Italy. Your face isn't that well known out there either. But look at you, you'll stand out a mile. Me? I just look like one of the old codgers.'

'He has a point,' said Jim. 'I'll need to make this formal in a few days, though. We have a duty of care to Susan. So you want to go in alone?'

'Yes. Send Jane and me off to Ireland. Week's holiday. Leave I have to take. That way, you can pick up my role,' said Macleod. 'You can deal with Ricci. Hope can be my liaison here. I can run things through her. She can report to you verbally. But we'll talk outside of police communications. Jane will be out of the way in Ireland. Everybody will think nothing of us being gone.'

'If you don't find anything within a couple of days—' said Jim.

'Give me five,' said Macleod.

'Four,' said Jim.

'So, we're saying at the moment that she's gone off on a week's leave and we're quite happy. Tell Ross,' said Macleod, 'that's the story he's got to go with. Okay? You can inform Perry, Hope. Don't inform Clarissa. Keep her team out of it. But tell Perry in case he gets a message. And if he does, he's to bring it straight to you.'

'He'll want to race out there as well,' said Hope.

'And if he does, he'll probably end up getting her killed. Or getting in trouble. Don't get me wrong; Perry's an excellent officer. But he won't work well out there.'

'I'll go with this,' said Jim. 'Okay? But I reserve the right to call it off. I reserve the right to bring everybody in, if I see fit.'

'Fair enough,' said Macleod. 'But use Hope. You've seen how well she works. You've seen that she understands situations.'

'Well, yes,' said Jim.

'Good,' said Macleod. 'I can leave you two then to hold things down here. I'm going to tell Jane she's going on holiday. Hope, you pick up the rest of the team.'

'When do you intend to go?' asked Jim.

'Go? I'm going in a couple of hours, as soon as I can get Jane organised. I'll be out there, hopefully by tomorrow morning at the latest.'

'Good,' said Jim. 'Best of luck, Seoras.' He leaned forward and shook the man's hand. 'You're going to need it.' Jim turned and left the room. Macleod looked back over at Hope behind the desk. He could see a frowning face.

'What?' he said. 'I need to go. I need to—'

'Look,' said Hope, 'I can handle myself if there's any violence. Yes, I get it. I'm a tall girl and I've got red hair and I'll stick out. Been sticking out for most of my life. But I can handle that.'

'I need to go,' said Macleod.

CHAPTER 10

'And you're going on your own? Seoras, you're over sixty.'
'And I've got years of experience, years of understanding.'
'Do you even speak Italian?' said Hope.
'No, barely spoken a word of Italian in my life. But I'm going.'
'You're obviously made up your mind on this, but take Ross with you, or Perry; take somebody with you.'
'No, this is off the books, and I won't do that to them, and I won't do that to you. If this blows up, well, what career did I have left anyway? A couple of years. You, you've got plenty left. You've got the family you want to start. You've got—'
'Don't give me that,' said Hope. 'You're doing this because you put her in this situation and you want to get her out. That's the long and the short of it, isn't it?'
Macleod nodded. 'We don't have time to discuss more,' he said. 'I'll be in touch. Hold the fort here. I might need you to keep Jim from going public on this. I'm banking on you for that.'
'You know I'm here. But make sure you get her. Get her home.'
Macleod nodded. He left the office, making his way back up to his own, the floor above. Once inside his own office, he picked up the phone and called Jane.
'What's up?' asked Jane.
'What do you mean, what's up?'
'You cut our lunch short, and then you're phoning me. You haven't been back in the office that long. Something is up.'
'We're going on holiday,' said Macleod. 'We're going to Ireland.'
'Really?'
'Yes, I've got a week's leave to take.' There was silence on the other end of the phone. 'What?' said Macleod. 'Do you not

like Ireland?'

'Ireland's brilliant,' she said. 'And we're definitely going to Ireland?'

'Oh, we're going to Ireland!' said Macleod.

'I'll get packed then,' she said. 'And weather-wise, you're going to need—'

'Pack for Ireland,' said Macleod. 'I'll speak to you soon. I won't be hanging about in the office.'

'Why? When are we going?'

'We hit the road tonight.'

'Seoras, what's up?'

'Later,' he said. 'Later.'

Macleod put the phone down, thankful that his partner understood life with him was always going to be strange. She stopped asking questions after a while, saying that he wouldn't answer them. Did he have secrets? Well, all relationships had secrets of some sort, even if it was only how he hated she cut her nails in the bathroom, leaving clippings everywhere. But that wasn't a real secret. Sometimes he had to keep real secrets from her, not talk about his work. She never pressed him for it, even if it inconvenienced her.

Macleod walked to his office door and locked it before returning to his desk. He took out a key and unlocked the bottom drawer of his desk, which was always locked. Inside, he fumbled around and found an envelope and took out a SIM card. He took his own phone, opened the rear, and placed the SIM card into the spare slot.

A lot of the officers had their private and police SIM on the same phone, running two cards. Macleod didn't have a private one. So, he put the sim into the empty slot. He closed the phone up, switched it back on, and waited. As he did so, he

CHAPTER 10

looked out of the window.

I've never been to Italy in my life, he thought. *One and a half legs. She was in trouble. How could she run? How could she get away? What was going on? I need to get to her quick.*

He had told Jim he was going on his own. He'd be undercover. The situation, as he saw it, could be very dire. Hope was totally correct. He was a sixty-year-old man. Yes, he had a brain. He knew how to use it. But he'd be off-territory here. He wouldn't have a team around him who could stave off any violence.

He looked at the phone, activated the sim that he'd put in, and made sure he was going to be dialling through it. It had one number on it, stored away in its contacts. It was just a number. There was nothing else with it.

Macleod called it, taking a deep breath as he did so. He'd need someone who could deal with violence. Someone who could deal with intrigue and undercover work. Someone who could deal with another government, if needs be. And someone who could get someone out of a problem fast, using contacts they'd have around the world.

A voice at the other end said, 'Hello.' Nothing more. Nothing less. No name.

'This is Seoras,' he said. 'I need your help. One of mine is in serious trouble. I need you now.'

'Where?'

'Italy. Rome.'

'Take down this address.' An email address was given. 'Send details to that address. Details of where you will be, where we can meet in Rome. Send it from a newly opened email account. And then, never use that account again, deleting the message once sent.'

'Thank you,' he said.

'See you soon,' was the only reply before the line went dead.

Macleod closed down his phone, took out the SIM card he'd previously put in, and cracked it. He then took half of the pieces and threw one in one bin, before popping outside and dispatching the rest of them in the secretary's bin. He came back inside and sat down at his desk.

Italy, he thought. His hands were sweating. If she was in trouble in Italy, he was truly going to a place where he would be out of his depth. *I'm coming, Susan*, he thought; *just hold on.*

Chapter 11

Macleod was exhausted. It had been full on, non-stop travel since he'd made the decision. They'd gone to Ireland, and he'd stopped at a small cottage with Jane, for barely an hour. While they'd been there, a Garda contact had dropped by, saying he would look after Jane.

Macleod had given instructions she was simply to enjoy herself, but keep a nice low profile, and ring Hope, if there were any problems. Hope would ring her, just to make sure she was okay. Macleod wasn't particularly worried about Jane, but he didn't know what he was going into. He always liked to make sure that his loved ones were well protected when he was stepping into the unknown.

Most criminal gangs didn't go after your loved ones. They went after you; you were the police, part of the job. However, he wasn't sure who he was dealing with. He also wasn't sure if there was a connection back to the UK.

Susan Cunningham had been following up on the death of Hamish Ferguson. Hamish Ferguson had been an academic in the UK for years. If something was up, maybe Hamish was embroiled. Macleod didn't know. But he wasn't going there to solve the case. He was going there to get Susan Cunningham out. Once that was done, he could raise merry hell about Hamish Ferguson and his case. There was no option until Susan was safe.

Macleod had thought about flying over, but he'd have to use his passport. He wasn't somebody with lots of connections and lots of false IDs. He was a Detective Chief Inspector, after all. Macleod rarely went off-piste. Certainly not like this. Yes, there was a time he'd been stepped down from the force, and yet still had gone down to Glasgow, backed up by Clarissa. But that was on the old turf. He wasn't working away from home then. This was different. He was going into alien territory. He didn't understand Italy, had no idea how they worked.

His Garda contact, however, had known a man with a boat. And Macleod had been dropped off at a harbour on the coast of Italy. From there, he caught a train into Rome, and now with a small amount of luggage, he stood at the train station.

It was dinnertime, for it had taken longer to get there than he'd hoped, but he didn't have time to rest. The library was the point of contact, the library from where the message had been sent. Susan had given nothing else. There was no other contact.

He'd emailed a very brief detail to his secret contact. There was no response, of course, no way for him to know if they were definitely on board. Whether they would meet him somewhere was unknown, but he wasn't to use that email address again. It was a shadowy world that they operated in but he would not wait for them either.

The library in Rome was a small one, and it was on the outskirts. And maybe that was a good thing. So, Macleod stuffed his luggage in the train station lockers before travelling

CHAPTER 11

on public transport to get to the library. He hoped Susan would send more messages from there because he didn't have a start point other than the library. Nowhere else to look for her, really. Not without going to the police. Not without investigating her short-term partner.

It would be hard for Macleod to maintain his low profile. His surmise at the moment was that Matteo was not involved, but was a good cop working with Cunningham. It made sense. But he had to be careful, because the other story could be that Susan was being got rid of by Matteo, part of the team. At some point, they would say that Susan had an accident. Maybe Matteo would instigate that accident.

Macleod now sat across a small Italian street. He was at a table in the cafe, sitting outside. The city had such a warm air, but the locals seemed to feel the chill, but not Macleod. He'd taken his coat off and left it over the chair.

A waitress came and asked him something, and he had no idea what she said. He hoped she was asking what he wanted. He picked up the menu and pointed to what he thought was coffee. Wasn't it just like home? What arrived was coffee, but it had milk in it, not black as he liked it. More like a French café au lait. He didn't complain, however, and simply sat sipping it, watching the library.

Susan was not about. He continued to sit there, realising he seemed to take a long time and do nothing. Macleod pulled out his phone and pretended to look at it, but in truth, he wasn't. He simply had the camera switched on.

The waitress came out again, and asked him what he thought was, 'Are you okay?' or 'Do you need anything else?' Macleod pointed to the menu. He thought it was pasta that would be coming. It looked like pasta. The menu had the pasta names on it. *Farfalle, Penn, Conchiglie. That was all pasta, wasn't it?*

He was relieved when twenty minutes later, a bowl of pasta arrived. He sat scoffing it. But as he did so, his keen eyes spotted something. The same group of people were going into the library. They were speaking to each other as they passed by, but quickly, quietly, not like they were friends. Then they headed inside the library.

Macleod finished his pasta, grabbed his coat, and left some Euros. He made his way over the road and stepped inside the ornate but quiet library. Like most libraries, there were books everywhere. But there was a librarian, with glasses pushed well up her nose, who stared at Macleod as he came in. He gave a smile and walked round, pretending to look at the architecture within, as well as the books.

He pulled out a book, opened it, and was taken aback by the pictures inside. There didn't seem to be a lot of clothing. He looked at the front cover of the book and realised it was something about photography. *The World of Glamour Photography*, he thought, that was what it was called. It was a wonderful cover, though.

Macleod would never be seen with a book like this in a library. He peered out from behind it, watching. The men who had seemed furtive outside were focused on a bank of computers towards the end of the library. Like most libraries, it seemed to have facilities for people. Maybe they were waiting for Susan.

Macleod was in the library for a couple of hours until he saw the librarian point to the clock. It must have been closing. He watched as the men disappeared, and hurriedly, he stepped outside. They went across to the cafe that he'd been sitting at previously, talking now to each other round a table, beer

CHAPTER 11

being consumed.

Macleod stepped inside the cafe, took up a table, and ordered himself something from the dessert menu. It was a cake when it arrived, but he'd had no idea. And he had another one of those milky coffees.

He felt slightly downcast. Here he was, there were people looking for someone, probably Susan, and she wasn't here. If she'd clocked them being here, would she remain? Would she go somewhere else? Because if she did, how was he going to find her in Rome, of all places?

He would struggle to find someone within London. Back home, he had all the resources. He could look at the CCTV, he could look at—he stopped. He couldn't be this negative, couldn't think what he couldn't do. No, he needed to think what he could do. What did he have?

Well, he had this group of men sitting at the tables before him. There were at least four of them. And every now and again, someone would come to the table, and someone else would disappear. Someone was sending messages. Someone knew about Susan's furtive emailing.

That was his surmise, so he needed to hang on to what evidence he had. And that was these men. He tried taking photographs of them without looking obvious, but Macleod wasn't a great wielder of a mobile phone. Ross was the one for that.

Slowly, one man got up, followed by another, leaving two at the table. Macleod left money for his food and drink and followed one of the men who had left. He'd try to get an address, and maybe watch it tomorrow, follow the man for where he went next.

Macleod walked along a distance behind the man, not

knowing where he was in Rome. He was loath to pull out a map, or even try to work that stupid one on the phone. If he looked like a tourist, it might blow his cover. Although he thought at the moment, he just looked like an elderly mute. He didn't want to open his mouth and give away who he was, but could he really play the old Italian? He wasn't sure.

The man turned down a side street, paint peeling from walls at the sides, shutters on the windows, balconies all the way up. Rome was very different to Glasgow or Inverness, and Macleod was feeling out of his depth.

He wondered how Jane was doing. She'd be worried sick about him, and she was probably right to be. He was so far from his comfort zone now, he couldn't believe it. He was impressed that Jim had let him come. Maybe he'd played his cards too much. Maybe Jim would fold before he got this sorted. Macleod gave his head a shake. 'Focus, Seoras,' he said. 'Focus. Where's the guy going?'

The man turned down an alleyway as the light was fading. Lamps were coming on as he turned left and then right, forcing Macleod to try to keep closer. When he turned round another corner, Macleod saw that the far end had a wall. It was simple stone. Flat, exquisitely carved.

There were no doorways down here. It was just a dead end and the man he'd been following.

Macleod froze. This man had taken him down here. Slowly, he looked back over his shoulder over a hundred metres to where the alleyway had run into this dead end. Behind him, he saw several men. They were the ones who had been sitting at the table.

Although it was dark, he could see that they carried knives. Not small flick knives either. They were closer to machete-

CHAPTER 11

sized. The men were young. Certainly, only mid-thirties. He turned and looked back at the man he'd been following. Macleod was outnumbered. And he was outgunned in terms of age. There was no doubt about it. There's nowhere to go, no doors to bang on down at this end of the alleyway.

'Maybe we could talk about this,' he said. And the man before him said something in Italian. Macleod believed that if he translated it, it would be two words, and the first one wouldn't be polite. His heart beat fast.

What was he doing here? How would he get out of this? He had no weapons. He hadn't wanted to be carrying weapons in a foreign country, in case he got searched, and then they'd stick him away somewhere. And besides, he didn't know how to use a weapon.

Macleod wasn't a fighter. He'd only ended up getting punched. That was why he had a team around him who could handle themselves. He was the brains of the outfit. But he wasn't the brains here. He walked into this one.

How had they been able to detect him? He was an old Italian. His clothes weren't Italian, though?

He offered up a prayer. Macleod had overstretched himself this time. He'd gone too far. How would he pay for it? He glanced over his shoulder. The men were getting closer. And the knives looked ever more threatening. One man made a motion across his own neck indicating he would slit Macleod's throat.

'English!'

'I'm Scottish!' said Macleod.

'We don't like English.'

I'm Scottish, thought Macleod. *I'm Scottish, not English.*

There was something welling up inside of him. He'd even die

being insulted. He had no problem with the English, having spent many hours working with several of them. But he hated to be called it. Even inside of him, that patriotic Scottishness flowed.

'Scottish,' he hissed. 'I'm Scottish.'

He raised his fists, preparing to take them on. He'd have to move quick; he'd have to hit them and run. Surely that was the only chance, or maybe he could talk. Maybe he could talk his way out of this. Macleod looked at the man's face; he looked at the knife; he cast a glance back at those coming down the alleyway towards him.

If you can talk yourself out of this one, Seoras, you should stand for First Minister.

Chapter 12

Macleod raised his hand. He needed to come up with some solution. Some way of stopping their approach.

'Can we talk?' he said. 'What is it you need? What is it you want from me? You don't like English. Who said I was English?'

The man in front of him just sneered and advanced. Macleod was sure they'd be on him within thirty seconds. Yet the single man was moving slower. Maybe so he would time his arrival at the same time as those from the rear were approaching Macleod.

There was nowhere to go, though. He looked around. Nowhere. Not even a doorway he could push open and get inside. He was caught out here. Completely caught out. He looked behind him again. He saw the three figures. But there was another figure there, approaching at speed. The man in front reached Macleod. The man's left arm came forward, the hand reaching for Macleod's shoulder.

Macleod could hear something behind him. There was a cry from one man. And somebody hit the wall. Hard. Macleod was sure a bone cracked as another cry split the air. Macleod turned round to look.

A small female figure was there, with a scarf pulled around her face and a baseball cap on. She grabbed another man, spun, and sent him careering into the wall. His head cracked off it, and he tumbled to the ground.

Macleod, however, was pulled forward by the man at the front who had advanced on him. A knife was whipped around in front of him, the blade across his throat. Macleod could do nothing, the speed at which everything was happening too much for him. He was disorientated, and a panic set in.

As he saw the knife before his throat, a hand from the woman reached up. It twisted the hand that held the knife hard. The knife fell instantly. The woman then stepped past Macleod, her other hand driving in under the ribcage of the other attacker, sending him backwards, sprawling to the ground.

She launched a kick behind her, catching another man in the gut as he came towards her. She spun, planting a hard fist into his face. The blood spattered off his nose and it sounded like it broke. The woman turned her attention back to the man at the front.

Once again she stepped forward, leaping, swinging two legs, one after the other, catching the man right under the chin, and sending him backwards. Macleod stood motionless, in awe of what was happening, until it was too late. He felt someone grab him. A heavy breath was in his ear.

He realised he'd been grabbed again by one of the men from behind, who the woman had taken out. A knife came up again, but this time the woman was too far away to react with her hand.

'I will kill him,' said the man.

His Italian accent was clear, but the English words were also articulated. 'Who are you?' the man asked the woman.

The woman peered back, her eyes penetrating, glaring at the knife. Her hands were being held up to either side, but having seen what she could do with them, Macleod didn't think they were at a point of surrender.

'You can walk,' said a voice he recognised. 'You can walk away.'

'What do you know?' asked the man. 'What do you know?'

'We know nothing,' said the woman, and then she was silent.

'What do you know?' the man asked in Macleod's ear. Blood had been pouring from the man's nose and some of it was now dripping on Macleod. He could hear the heavy breathing of the man, still reeling from the punches that had been landed by the woman.

'If you know nothing, then we should get rid of you,' said the man. Beside him, a couple of his colleagues were getting back to their feet. 'Get rid of you both,' said the man, 'starting with this one.'

Time seemed to slow for Macleod. The man's arm pulling across, the blade heading towards Macleod's neck. The stunning speed of the woman, reaching and pulling a gun from somewhere. And then there were two gunshots, but both were silenced.

Macleod would realise afterwards there was a barrel at the front of the gun that took away the sound, leaving a rather dull puff. The man holding the knife, however, suddenly spun off Macleod, blood spattering. He whipped backwards and Macleod turned to see him falling. Macleod was then grabbed under the arm and dragged along, almost casually.

The woman's spare arm was whipped out and struck one of the other men across the jaw, sending him spinning again, clattering into the wall. Macleod felt his feet stumbling along as he was dragged up the alleyway.

'Move, just move,' said the voice beside him.

They approached the edge of the alleyway, and as they turned the corner, three more men were standing there. They all had knives, none of them with guns, and the woman put the gun away, letting go of Macleod. She stepped forward, and he witnessed the flurry of punches as she wove, ducked and dived, and then stood there, some twenty seconds later, waving Macleod on.

The three men had careered to all sides of the alleyway and were lying on the floor. Macleod stumbled forward, almost in a daze. His mind was going back to the man who had been shot, the one who had been holding the knife at his throat. There had been no hesitation from the woman. Something Macleod struggled to grasp.

But she was grabbing his arm again, pulling him along. They cut down one alleyway, and then another one. And all the time she kept her mask up. Macleod wondered if he'd be pulled onto public transport, but the woman seemed to want to stay clear of everyone. Everywhere she went, she was cutting down alleyways or back streets.

A woman came out with her washing, and the pair of them nearly clattered into her. Macleod went to apologise, but he was dragged along too quickly. He was taken down through an archway by some water, round the side of it and up through another archway.

He then thought they were running through people's rear gardens. They looked more spectacular than any gardens he'd been in. And then they cut through another place, down some steps, and then peered at the back of a tall building. Macleod was hurried up some iron steps, in through a wooden door. The door was closed behind, another door was opened, and Macleod was half-pushed, half-flung onto a sofa.

'Stay there,' said the voice.

Macleod watched as the woman made her way to the window, checked outside, then closed the curtains. She then ducked back out of the room, and he heard her disappearing outside. A full five minutes later, she walked back into the room.

Macleod was shaking. As he sat on an old, probably disused sofa, the stuffing coming out on one side, he smelt the fustiness of the room. It hadn't been lived in for a long time.

The woman was now standing before him. She'd been wearing a black jacket, not leather, but certainly waterproof, and she unzipped it, placing it down on the floor beside her. Her arms were sweating, and the part of her face he could see looked deeply flushed. She reached up, taking off her baseball cap, laying it to one side as the long hair unravelled itself, falling down by her side onto her shoulders. She reached back, untied the scarf, and let it drop to the floor. Macleod looked up at the face he knew. Kirsten Stewart.

Kirsten Stewart had worked with Macleod first on the Isle of Lewis as a uniformed constable before joining the murder team as a detective constable. After a significant time with him, Macleod had urged her to take up with the Secret Service.

And she'd gone. And though he'd kept contact with her, most recently she'd had to depart. Something big had gone down within the Service. Something Macleod didn't fully understand and Kirsten had gone. She was only around five feet four, but she was an incredibly fit specimen, muscly and yet very feminine.

She was still young, under thirty, but Macleod could see that the recent past had taken a toll on her eyes. He'd known she'd loved and lost in some of the most horrific ways possible, but the finer details he didn't know. She was now standing in black hiking boots, green trousers and a black crop top. She pulled her hair backwards, running her fingers through it, before staring at him again.

'Seoras,' she said. 'What the hell?'

'What do you mean?' he said.

'I barely got you out of there! I mean, what the hell?' she turned, almost stomping off to the corner of the room, before turning back.

'Didn't you get my report?' he said. 'I sent you all the details I had.'

'You came to ask for my help. I thought you would wait for me to arrive.'

'How?' said Macleod. 'You didn't give me any details. I haven't got any way to contact you. You haven't—'

'I would find you,' she said. 'I found you easily.'

'How?'

'You said the library. First place you'd go to look. Message came from the library. Course you'd be there.'

'I didn't see you,' said Macleod.

'Of course you didn't,' said Kirsten. She shook her head. 'I can't believe you're so stupid.'

'Don't you call me stupid,' said Macleod.

'Whoa. You may have been the boss one day,' said Kirsten, 'but I am now. This is my world. Understand? It's taken me time to learn it. I've had hard times within it, but this is my world. I know it, I live it, I breathe it. You don't.'

'Whose is this place anyway?' said Macleod. 'It's not been—'

CHAPTER 12

'It's not been lived in for three years,' said Kirsten. 'It's not mine, it's a contact's. We have places around the world.'

'Around the world,' said Macleod. 'You were disappearing, you were—'

'Yes,' she said. 'And I gave you a number in case you were ever in trouble. Because, because you're my friend. Because you were my mentor. You shouldn't be here,' she said.

'I have to be here. One of my people's missing.'

'Susan Cunningham, you said.'

'She's obvious,' said Macleod. 'She's only got half a leg.'

'But if you wear the trousers and the prosthetic, surely it doesn't show much,' said Kirsten.

'She hasn't had a prosthetic yet.'

Kirsten stopped for a moment and looked at Macleod. 'You're telling me she's on the run here, and she's missing half a leg, and she's got no prosthetic; she's got no way to cover that up, to—'

'No,' said Macleod.

'Seoras, what have you got us into?'

'I don't know. All I know is I need her out.'

Kirsten shook her head and left the room. Macleod didn't know what to make of it. In the past, whenever he'd met Kirsten, they'd always been, convivial at worst. Usually chatty. Usually. He would want to know as much detail, whatever she could tell him. Which usually wasn't a lot, given that she'd worked for the Secret Service. Now, instead, she was out on her own. Which was why he called her.

'You picked up a lot of heat,' said Kirsten. 'What were you thinking?'

'I was being an old man in Rome. I was—'

'When have you ever done much undercover? When have

you ever gone into a foreign culture?'

'I haven't,' he said. 'That's why I was calling you, but I couldn't wait. I needed to . . .'

'Sometimes you have to wait, Seoras,' said Kirsten. 'This game's different.' She turned and walked over to the sofa. Putting her hands down, which he took, she pulled him to his feet. Kirsten wrapped her arms around him.

'You're a daft idiot,' she said, 'but it really is so very good to see you again.'

Chapter 13

Macleod looked up at Kirsten. He couldn't believe the question, let alone the fact she was asking it.

'It's a simple question,' she said. 'Do I need to eliminate those I incapacitated back there?'

'What do you mean?' asked Macleod.

'You know what I mean. Do I need to put them to sleep properly?'

'We're away from them. We're—'

'They know you're here. They know I'm involved. In my work, you don't leave people behind talking unless you want to.'

'I'm not in your line of work,' said Macleod testily. He was feeling all akilter. Only recently, it looked like he might die, his throat slit. Memories of Patterson, and what had happened to him, came flooding back, and Macleod was having cold sweats. His hands were feeling numb.

'Do I need to go out and despatch these people?' said Kirsten. 'What do they know about you?'

'I don't even know if they know me. I'm not very popular around here.'

'This is serious, Seoras. It could have implications for people at home. Do we even know who these people are?'

'I don't,' said Macleod. 'But they were watching. They were huddled round that library, then they were inside. They were looking for somebody to use that computer. And that is the place the text message was sent from to Hope. Susan Cunningham had been here.'

'So how did they know?'

'What do you mean?' asked Macleod.

'How did they know?' said Kirsten. 'Did somebody inform them? Is it because they knew she was close by?'

'I don't know how they knew,' said Macleod.

'Right. Well then, we need to think more carefully about this.'

'Can't you just bring in the Service?' asked Macleod.

'Why didn't you?' said Kirsten. 'I'm not with them anymore.'

'No, but you'll have contacts. You'll be able to ask Anna Hunt.'

'The Service went into turmoil, Seoras. Anna Hunt's trying to get it back on its feet. I left. I was in South America. You were just lucky I wasn't out of mobile contact. And you said it was important, so I came.'

'But can't you talk to Anna Hunt? We're in a foreign country. She could organise something.'

'Anna Hunt will not look kindly on us operating in a foreign country, completely unsupervised. I've had to operate in other places before, but as part of British government activity. The one time I went off-piste, because I had to, they weren't impressed by it.'

'Well, you can call her, can't you?' said Macleod.

'She will not entertain what you're doing, okay? She really won't like the fact that I'm involved, because I'm a lone wolf.'

CHAPTER 13

'Well, we need to do something,' said Macleod. 'We need to work out what we're doing here. We need more manpower.'

'Stop. First off, Seoras, go home,' said Kirsten. 'You're in your sixties. You're in no condition to charge around here.'

'But I can help. I know Susan Cunningham, know how she thinks. I know—'

'Hang on a minute,' said Kirsten. 'Can I just get this into your head? You're not a detective chief inspector here. It's not a case that you just simply demand to have things happen and they happen. There's no process to follow here. And you're off piste. Can you tell me how many people back home know about this?'

'The ACC does. But he's keeping under his hat. Hope knows as well.'

'And you say the ACC's keeping it under his hat? For how long? How long does that go on and how long does it get before people start to get worried about what you're doing? You can't kick up a fuss.'

'Wait, they kicked up a fuss at me.'

'Look, even if we assume you're right, the Italians will not want a couple of Scots to come over and point out all their irregularities and put it in the press.'

'I don't care about that,' said Macleod. 'I just want her back. And that's going to be the game.'

'And I will do it. But not with you.'

'I'm staying anyway,' spat Macleod.

'Fine,' said Kirsten. 'Walk out the door, and off you go. See how far you get. If I hadn't had been there, you'd be dead. Understand? Dead!'

'I realise that. Thank you.'

'Don't thank me. Learn from it. Now I'm going out for a

couple of hours, and I'll see if I can pick up some information. Where's your luggage? I take it you have some. You didn't just come in that outfit.'

'It's at the train station, in a locker.'

'I'll bring it back,' said Kirsten. 'Make sure nobody's following you or is watching for you. Make sure they haven't spotted you coming in.'

Macleod sat alone in the small flat. He found himself standing up, walking to one side of the room, entering the kitchen with its small number of utensils. He made himself coffee, then sat back down again.

Macleod wanted to go outside, find a coffee shop, sit down and think. That's where he worked best, not stuck in a room like this. He wondered where Kirsten was. He thought meeting her again would be, well, more civil than this. She was like a favourite daughter. She had been one of his prized pupils. Now Kirsten was very different.

Macleod felt clammy and stood up. He put a hand to his forehead. He was sweating profusely. His mind spun, thinking about how close he'd been to death. The man had gone to slice his throat. It was only Kirsten's incredible reaction and quick shot that stopped him.

Macleod stumbled back onto the sofa and tears streamed down his face. He had said goodbye to Jane but not like that, not to have disappeared, not to have—he shivered. He wasn't cold. This was Italy. It was warm. But inside, he was a mess.

He almost jumped out of his skin when the door opened for he had heard no one approach. But as he looked up, he saw it was Kirsten and breathed a sigh of relief.

'Well, it's got interesting,' said Kirsten.

'What do you mean?' asked Macleod.

CHAPTER 13

'There's been many people asking for a disabled woman from Scotland. Blonde hair. Been round the information peddlers and made a few of them speak.

'So, has anybody seen her?'

'There's talk that she was with an Italian man, Matteo. I don't know if that's a genuine report or if that's been put out there. You said that Inspector said that she'd gone off with Matteo for a week's holiday.'

'That's what he said. Don't believe it for a minute,' said Macleod.

'Well, that's fair enough,' said Kirsten. 'But it's not helping us any, is it? If we're going to find your Susan Cunningham, we're going to have to run down the leads that she's left behind. If she went away with Matteo, he could be the bet to go for.'

'Because?'

'He's Italian, from here and will have history. He'll have people with grudges. People who'll talk about him. Nobody here knows Susan. She's just the amputee from Scotland. Matteo is our best bet. He has history in the city.'

'So how do we do that, then?' asked Macleod.

'We get his address, we get his home life. We see where he is. I mean, is anybody missing him? Is anybody annoyed that he's gone away? Things like that.'

'What about Hamish Ferguson?' asked Macleod.

'What about him?'

'She was investigating his links to our history and his death.'

'I'm not your historian here. I'm not Indiana Jones. Okay? My job is to get your Susan Cunningham out of here. Back to the UK. Once that's done, I'm out, Seoras. Understand me? And you're back with her. What's going on with the rest of it, the Italians can look after that.'

'Or can they?' he said. 'Doesn't look like to me. They seem to be part of the problem. There may be a—'

'Hold it! Okay?' said Kirsten. 'What are you asking me to do here? If there's corruption running through the Italian authorities, the Italian authorities will have to sort it out. We have no jurisdiction. When I worked for the Service, I wasn't coming back with a solution for everything. I was tasked with specific things. Discover specific things. To stop leaks. To find where someone was and get them out. Specific jobs. Not general investigations.

'You want to investigate what happened to this Hamish Ferguson? That's detective work. Nothing you can do about it. Needs to be done by the people within the country, not me. The only detective work I'm doing is to find out where Susan Cunningham is. When we get her, both of you are getting out of this country by the fastest method possible. And then I'll talk to Anna Hunt so you don't leave the UK again.'

Macleod shook his head. He stood up, went through over to the window, and went to pull back the curtains.

'What are you doing? No curtains! This place, this is where you stay, okay?' said Kirsten. 'You don't put your head out there. Four guys knew you. One's dead. The other three are up on their feet again. Your face becomes known. That's why I asked you if I needed to despatch them. I know you find that unpalatable.'

'You would have found it unpalatable once upon a time,' said Macleod.

'Can I remind you that you put me into the service,' said Kirsten. 'We operate on different bits of the law, above it, around it, help protect it.'

'Don't lecture me,' said Macleod.

CHAPTER 13

'Why not? You're the one who needs me,' said Kirsten. 'Keep away from that damn window!'

Macleod turned and walked back to the sofa. He felt useless. She turned back to him.

'Look, Seoras, you're way out of your depth here, far from where you normally work. You're far from home and got no buddies. You've got me. We will find her. Dead or alive, we'll find her,' said Kirsten solemnly.

'Did you have to shoot him?' said Macleod suddenly.

'Who?' asked Kirsten.

'The man. The man who was holding me.'

'He put a knife to your throat. I wasn't shooting anybody, if you noticed, before that. But I wouldn't have got there in time. You'd be dead. So, I killed him.'

'And that's it,' said Macleod. 'You just killed him. You don't—'

'I don't what? Care? Feel nothing? Oh, I feel it. But I feel it at a different time. He's dead. And I can justify why I did it. I justify everything I do. Work it out.'

'You justify it. But nobody else justifies it for you, do they? We can justify anything to ourselves.'

'Yes, we can,' said Kirsten sharply. 'You justified hauling your arse out here to come and find Susan Cunningham, when you were far from the best-placed person. I bet you told Hope she should stay. Hope's a tall redhead. She'd be so obvious. Whereas the Scottish detective isn't? I mean, you don't even look like an old Italian man. You dress like a UK man. You dress like somebody from Scotland. Don't know if you've noticed, but the weather's better here. They change what they do, they dress differently, they eat different food. You just don't look like an Italian man.'

'Well, I'm here. I'm not leaving.'

'I'll take you out of this country in the next couple of hours. Not a problem,' said Kirsten.

'It is a problem,' said Macleod. 'Cunningham's still here.'

'And I'll deal with that. And I'll get her out of here,' said Kirsten. 'But at the moment, you're in the way. You're cramping me. You're not helping.'

'But you need me. Nobody else understands Cunningham like me.'

'Well, we're going to keep you off the streets as much as possible.' She turned and looked away and turned back again. 'You don't speak Italian, do you? I saw you in the coffee shop pointing at the menu. You don't speak Italian. Why would you come? What is the point of this? Is your ego so big you think you can solve everything?'

'At the moment, I don't feel I can even look after myself here. I can't even order a coffee without pointing at random at some menu,' he said. It came out of the blue and cut Kirsten to her core. 'Okay. We need to recoup. We need to plan. I get that.'

'You need to go home,' said Kirsten. She stepped forward and Macleod stood up. She hugged him. 'You need to go home. I can't risk losing you here because you're daft enough to be here. Okay. Why don't you just go home? It'll work out better if you just go home. You do realise that?'

'You don't understand the way the detective world works. You don't understand about corruption. When did you ever work on any corruption cases?' asked Macleod.

'What are you saying?' asked Kirsten.

'If this has got corruption, I'll smell it. I'll be able to find it out because I understand how corruption works. You need me to analyse which means you need me to be here. You don't want me on the street? Fine. You know that side of things, so

CHAPTER 13

you cover that off. We'll manage.'

'The only reason you're here is for her. You feel guilty, Seoras. You can't feel guilty. It makes you slow, sluggish. You want to stay? Fine. But if we do, it's my rules. And if I tell you, you're out, you're out. If it's too hot, you go. If I tell you to stay in here, you stay. You're not the boss on this one, Seoras. I am! I call the shots! You agree with that?'

'I do,' he said, sitting down again. Kirsten watched as his hands shook.

'Is that the first time you've—'

'No. I've seen people die before,' said Macleod. 'The problem is that, well, it gets no easier.'

'Trust me, it doesn't get any easier killing them. Now make me a coffee,' she said. Macleod looked up. 'My rules. Coffee!'

Chapter 14

Macleod awoke inside Kirsten's temporary accommodations and found that she was gone. He thought about leaving the building to see what he could discover. But if she was gone, she'd have been gone for a reason. She had set out her rules, and he was going to have to abide by them. It wasn't easy, though.

Macleod was used to the idea of running a team. At the very least, their ideas were vetted before him. So even if he wasn't in charge, he was giving a steadying hand on the ship. Here, he felt he wouldn't have that privilege. He got up and washed, though, before going through his clothing and putting on what he thought looked less respectable than normal.

It was ten minutes after this that the door of the flat opened and Kirsten came in with a shopping bag.

'Where have you been?' asked Macleod.

'Information gathering. I found Matteo's apartment. Apparently, Susan and he were as thick as thieves. He was at her hotel with her.'

'She was assigned to work the case with him. She never said he was anything but appropriate and intelligent.'

'That may be so, Seoras,' said Kirsten. 'We've got to be careful

CHAPTER 14

here. We don't know if he's a bad guy or not. I've got his apartment's address. We'll see what we can do. I need to get in, see what sort of person he was.'

'You want to break into his apartment? But if you do that, you won't be able to use any—'

'This isn't evidence gathering,' said Kirsten quickly. 'We're beyond that. Primary issue is the safety of Susan Cunningham. Secondary issue is what's going on. You've tasked me with an extraction. This is not a police investigation.'

'Clearly it is. Especially if it's police corruption.'

'No, Seoras,' said Kirsten. 'If it's police corruption that we're bothered about, we contact the Italian authorities and ask them to get on with it. This is an extraction because we're worried about the safety of one of our people. Nothing more, nothing less. Whatever we find out is the truth beyond that is secondary and only of interest in finding out where she's gone.

'For now, we need to find out the person she's alleged to be with. Now, Matteo is either working against her—in which case we're in real trouble if we don't find him—or he's genuine. In that case, whoever has decided to shift Susan out of the way, will shift him out of the way too. Either way, his place will be watched. We'll have to be careful.'

'So how do we get in?' asked Macleod.

'You don't,' she said.

'I know you said you were in charge, but I didn't expect to stand in the wings.'

'You don't because you aren't fit for that operation.' She looked over at him and he saw eyes filled with a tinge of sorrow. 'You sent me down a path, Seoras, into a different world. When I break into this apartment, nobody will see me. Nobody will know I've been in. What I need you to be is my lookout man. I need somebody down below, just in case someone comes up to the apartment. In order to do this, I got you some clothes.'

'What do you mean "you got me some clothes?"'

'So you can actually look like an Italian man, not some British tourist. An older British tourist at that.' Kirsten gave Macleod a bag of clothing. 'You need to change into that. Grease your hair.'

'What?'

'Grease your hair. The older Italians style their hair, grease it back when they're older.'

'Why?'

'It doesn't matter why,' said Kirsten. 'You're here to fit in, so fit in, but don't speak to anyone.'

'So what do I do?' asked Macleod.

'Shrug your shoulders and pretend you don't know. Worst-case scenario, tap your ear. Pretend you're half deaf. Won't be that far away from the truth.'

Macleod started, then realised that she was winding him up.

'You be careful going in. I want to hear everything when you come back.'

'Of course,' said Kirsten. 'The reason you're still here is because of your brain.'

'The reason I'm still here is that I told you I wasn't leaving,' said Macleod.

'If you seriously think that'll stop me from making you go,' said Kirsten, 'you've got another thought coming. I love you too much to be sentimental about this.'

Macleod stared at her. 'What's that meant to mean?' he said.

'We're on foreign soil,' said Kirsten. 'I haven't got back up. The last thing I want is you going down here. If Susan

Cunningham's been involved in something or got herself into something, and ends up . . . dead, well, you know, we tried. Didn't have the option of stopping it before it started.

'With you, however, I do have that option, but I need your mind. You were always sharp. You could always see the other side of things. And also this police corruption. You'll have seen enough of it in your time. Seoras, you sold me on that. You'll understand how these characters work. It's not what I do.'

Kirsten turned away to allow Macleod to change. And when he'd done so, they headed out into the blazing sunshine of Rome. Kirsten kept to the back streets, out-of-the-way places, far from busy crowds. She didn't take a taxi or a bus, but instead, they walked some three miles before they got to Matteo's apartment.

It was a classy area, swish little restaurants and diners here. A gym. Art shops. Ones that Macleod thought Clarissa would love. Although he couldn't tell if anything in them was worth anything. *Clarissa*, he thought. *She would be waiting for him to return calls. Would she be appeased by the lie he was in Ireland? Well, she'd just have to wait. He didn't have time.'*

The apartment was across the road, some one hundred metres away, on the fifth floor. Kirsten went to a coffee shop and told Macleod to sit down and came back with a coffee for him. She placed a bunch of cigarettes in front of him, too.

'Smoke those and keep your eye out, okay? Here,' she handed him something. 'Stick that in your ear. It's switched on. All you've got to do is say quietly what you want me to hear.'

'Okay,' said Macleod. 'But—'

'No buts unless they're from the cigarettes,' she said, as she placed something into his jacket.

'What's that?'

'That's the microphone that's going to pick up what you're saying. Remember, it's live now. I can hear everything you say. So when I'm up there, don't sit and waffle. Don't talk out loud to yourself. Just sit with a coffee and holler if anybody comes.'

'What do you mean by holler? Like, shout.'

'No. Just quietly sit here. I'll be about an hour, maybe an hour and a half.'

'You realise I don't smoke,' said Macleod.

'You do now,' she said. 'Smokers stay longer, especially ones that are sitting down with their coffee. If you need to order another one, just raise your hand and point at the drink. Say nothing, okay?'

'What if they ask?'

'Finger, drink, point,' said Kirsten. 'Trust me, they'll think you're just some sort of miserable sod.'

'Cheers,' said Macleod.

Kirsten was off, leaving his coffee in front of him, and then disappearing out onto the street. Macleod never saw her near the building once. He didn't hear anything from her. Maybe the open channel was only from him to her. Maybe she had more control.

'Entering,' came a voice.

'Roger,' said Macleod.

He sat and looked up and down the street. People were walking here, there, and everywhere, unaware that DCI Macleod was on their turf. What would happen if he got caught? That couldn't happen, could it? But that's why Kirsten was here. She knew how to handle these things.

As much as it peeved him, he was glad that she was with him. Not only because she'd probably saved his life, but also

CHAPTER 14

because he wasn't good at this. He rarely went undercover. He didn't break into places without a warrant. There were people on his team who did that, sometimes. Not that he ever asked them about it.

'Extracting.'

'What?' said Macleod quietly.

'Extracting. I'm on my way out.'

'Roger.'

This was so different to the police, completely against authority and procedure. He realised he'd been quite rash about going over, but he thought that Susan Cunningham's life was in real danger. Being so far from home, something was wrong. It could take weeks to set it up diplomatically. Would anybody else have got into it? He truly believed she'd be dead once any significant heat was put on. Macleod wasn't having that. He had sent Susan here; he'd bring her back.

'You can leave now. I'm round the corner.'

Macleod had seen nothing of Kirsten at the building, but he put out a cigarette that he was failing to smoke. He stood up and marched around the edge of the building to see Kirsten in the alleyway.

'How'd it go?' he asked.

'Shush,' she said. 'Not till we're back. Follow me.'

Macleod puffed as Kirsten set off at a good pace. She only slowed when she encountered company. And then, once clear, she picked her pace up again. By the time they got back into the temporary accommodation, Macleod was exhausted. She locked the door behind him when he entered, turned several locks, and told him to sit down on the sofa.

'I'll do the coffee,' she said.

'I can do that. You've been busy.'

'Stop it,' she said. 'You're tired; you're exhausted. I kept a fair pace going on the way back. I know that. Okay? Don't be brave. Try to be thoughtful. Pick up on what's going on.'

Macleod collapsed, closed his eyes, and then heard a coffee being placed down on a table, causing him to open them again. Kirsten was sitting beside him. She was buzzing.

He remembered what he truly liked about her. The way she was, the long black hair, the punchy spirit, ready to take on the world. And yet her eyes seemed somewhat darker these days. There was somewhere behind them he wasn't allowed to go. Somewhere she kept locked up tight.

He knew about her losing Craig, her lover. But there was something more these days. Something he didn't understand. And he wasn't about to ask her now.

'Most of his place was normal. Run of the mill stuff. Magazines. Looks like he's quite the young man around town. Seems to enjoy himself. Fit, healthy lifestyle, given the number of sports rackets and things he had,' said Kirsten. 'But he also had a secret place, a hidden compartment.'

'Just the one,' said Macleod jokingly.

'Three,' said Kirsten. 'Two of them were empty. But the one that wasn't had all this in it. I think the others have been opened. Somebody's been through his place. The compartment holding these goods was much harder to locate.'

'Let's see it then.'

Kirsten put down a large manila file with lots of sheets of paper in it.

Macleod eagerly took them out and laid them down on the coffee table in front of him. He began reading through. Kirsten started from the other side.

'What's the order of Calgacus?' asked Macleod.

CHAPTER 14

'New one on me,' said Kirsten. 'Never heard of it.'

'Calgacus was mentioned by Susan briefly,' said Macleod. 'Have you got internet?'

'Use this tablet,' said Kirsten. 'They won't trace it.'

Macleod took the tablet off Kirsten and started tapping in on Google search.

'Calgacus is a Scottish warrior. Caledonian. Fighting back. But the order of Calgacus? It's not here,' he said. He began reading on through the notes.

'According to Ferguson, it's a group. The Order of Calgacus. Why would anybody have a group formed around this guy? He's ancient,' said Macleod, 'and he was also defeated. Badly.'

'And that somehow stops people from forming around him? We come from Scotland. To rise up and be a nation again? Like the anthem says.'

'Well,' said Macleod. 'I get stopping other people coming into your country, but . . . he says that the Order of Calgacus is eminent in this city. In Rome. Why?'

'Does he say anything else?'

'His boss, Ricci, is involved, but he doesn't know to what extent. That makes it tough for him. I can assume, then, that he's not someone who got rid of Susan. Maybe she's trying to help him,' said Macleod.

'You assume nothing,' said Kirsten. 'Three hidden areas, two empty, one wasn't. This could be a drop, this could be there for us.'

'What do you mean, there for us?'

'Doesn't work like when we were police. There's a lot of subterfuge that goes on. They might have emptied the place, and then put that in to say that Matteo was alongside Susan to throw us off.'

'That makes little sense though, because at the moment, he's tied into it. It says here,' continued Macleod, 'that there's a number of possible initiates in the Order.'

'The Order's recruiting? How big is it?' asked Kirsten.

'It doesn't say here,' advised Macleod, 'but he thinks his best bet, according to this, is going after a priest, Father Dominic Conti.'

'Does it say anything else about him?'

'He works in the papal offices in the Vatican City,' said Macleod.

'Well, we won't be meeting him in there. If Matteo's on the level, and there is this group running around, and he thinks that Father Conti is part of the group, then he's very much worth going after,' said Kirsten. 'But we don't do it suddenly. We go find him, we ask him.'

'What?' said Macleod. 'We can't just bring him in and interview him.'

'We won't be interviewing him. We'll put him under pressure and get what we need.'

'I'm not condoning any sort of torture.'

'What?' said Kirsten. 'I'm not saying you should. Look, what do you think I am?'

'You're not the woman that left me, far from the woman that I thought I knew. Kirsten, you dispatched somebody right beside me and you—'

'You'd be dead if I didn't,' said Kirsten. 'This world we're in, you're going to have to get used to the idea that you might have to do something dirty, something you don't like. I've killed a few people in my time, Seoras, but I can live with it, because they deserved it. Father Dominic Conti, he may deserve it; we'll see, but what we need to do is find out when he's going

CHAPTER 14

to be outside the Vatican.'

Chapter 15

Macleod spent most of the day stuck in the temporary accommodation, Kirsten having gone out. She left Macleod to ponder over the evidence she collected from Matteo's address.

From what he could make out from Matteo's writing, for some of it was in Italian, the order of Calgacus had been spreading. Macleod was thankful that Matteo had written a lot in English. He wondered why. He would take this up with Kirsten when she returned.

Maybe it was because of Susan coming out. Susan could speak Italian very well, but to read Italian. It's one reason Macleod thought this job would have suited her. But Matteo may not have known that or may not have thought she'd be up to it. After all, most people who learnt the language didn't speak like locals. Did he intend to give her this information once he'd checked out just who she was?

If these statements from Matteo—these deductions—were genuine, he was clearly looking to bring down those who were involved. Ricci, his boss. *Matteo would have to be so careful*, thought Macleod, *to bring down your own boss while working for him. What was he doing? How was he doing it? Did Susan know? If Susan knew, why wouldn't she tell Macleod? Or had she? Indirectly.*

After all, you couldn't just say it. Everything was likely to be checked. Phone calls made from hotels or offices. Maybe she was being watched. He had no idea what pressure Susan had been under. All he knew was that she'd sent a message to Hope on a personal account, via a library. He stopped for a moment, thinking about Susan.

How on earth was she getting about? On a crutch, on the run. She's tenacious. In that way, she's like Hope. But Susan isn't Hope. She's different. Hope would have come in with this. Hope would have taken this to the highest and dumped it in front of him. Susan isn't there yet. She is very, very far from that position. At least she's a good copper. But this is way above her pay grade. It's above my pay grade, if I'm honest.

Macleod received a phone call on the special SIM card given to him by Kirsten. She advised Macleod that she'd traced Conti that night going out to a small restaurant in a quiet part of Rome. She passed on the address and told Macleod to be there by nine o'clock.

As it was a restaurant, Macleod dressed in a shirt and tie but left off his coat. He had been wearing a larger coat, but thought it would be less obvious that he was an inspector without it. He almost put his hat on. *How many men were walking around here in fedoras at night?* None, he remembered seeing.

The taxi, caught on the street several streets from their accommodation, drove through Rome, and Macleod looked at the busy streets. It might have been a weekday evening, but everybody seemed to be out. European cities were different, weren't they? These late-night meals, half of them taken out beside the street. There was less yobbishness. Not that there was that much in Inverness.

Though he enjoyed going out for meals with Jane, they weren't like this, wandering the streets and popping into a quiet cafe. But this was a younger crowd, wasn't it? He noticed an older man sitting with an older woman outside one of the cafe-cum-restaurants. No, he thought, *this is just a way of life.*

The taxi driver pulled over, and Macleod, without saying a word, handed him some notes, wondering if it was enough. The man didn't seem to complain, but smiled and indicated he could write a receipt. Macleod shook his head. He would have loved to have taken the receipt and claimed the money back, but there could be no traces. Kirsten had called for the taxi to make sure it had been delivered in good Italian.

As he stepped out from the vehicle, he felt somebody passing by, touching his shoulder. And a voice said, 'That's me, down to the left.'

He felt like a child. He remembered when he was instructing Kirsten on what to do, when he was the one leading the investigation. The days when her fists and her strength were what he needed her for. Things hadn't really changed, had they? And yet she must have needed him, because he was still here.

'I'm going to make sure that the restaurant's available for just us before our priest arrives. When he does, you question him.'

'What if he doesn't speak English?'

'Father Dominic Conti is an Irish priest, Seoras. Not everybody here in Rome comes from Rome. Certainly not everybody in the Vatican City.'

'He works in the papal offices,' said Macleod.

'That's right,' said Kirsten. 'Seems like the order's getting people high in certain places. The church would be an obvious one to get people into over here. There's a lot of sway. Much more than back home.'

'Church doesn't have enough sway on people,' said Macleod. Kirsten gave him a look.

'I find the church does bad things at times.'

'I didn't mean the church. I meant—'

'I know you meant God. While I'd love to sit down and have an evangelical and possibly theological discussion with you, we don't have time, Seoras, okay? Wait here. And if Conti comes in, follow him.'

'How do I know it's Conti?'

'He's Irish. He's a priest,' said Kirsten. 'You'll spot him getting out of a taxi. He'll be one without a gaggle of women around him.'

Macleod smiled. She was joking again. While he stood on the street corner, she disappeared inside the restaurant. Macleod didn't hear any sound coming from the restaurant but he noticed that nobody was coming back out. Had it been busy? He wasn't sure. Maybe not.

Conti was coming to meet someone. How had she known? She hadn't told him. Was she tapping Conti's calls? Was she making plans without Macleod? Had she broken into the Vatican? Macleod's mind raced. This was her world, not his.

A car pulled up and a man stepped out. He had a small purple hat on, a flat cloth but a coat wrapped up around him. Macleod thought he could see a priest's garments underneath. The man didn't turn round and thank the driver. He simply ignored him as the driver drove off. Macleod followed this priest in entering the room behind him. The restaurant was empty. There was a table and there was Kirsten.

'Father Dominic Conti, I presume,' said Kirsten. 'Good. Need to have a word with you.'

'Who are you?' snapped the man.

'You don't need to put on the Italian voice. You can speak in your home Irish. Not from there, but I think I've got a good, reasonable grasp of it.'

The man spoke in Irish Gaelic, and Macleod could pick up most of it.

'There's no need to insult her,' said Macleod. 'Because if you do again, she may well break something. Sit down!'

The priest went to turn to walk out, and Macleod went to intercept him. Before he could, Kirsten was on her feet, and grabbed the priest by the collar, lifting him off his feet, and dumped him in a chair.

'Sit,' she said. 'Do I have to tie you up, or are you going to be a good boy?'

The man looked deeply annoyed. He went to raise his hand to Kirsten, but she simply grabbed his wrist and twisted it. The man yelped.

'I don't want to break it, because then we have to go through all the explanations,' she said. 'But if you give me any more problems, I will break it. You will talk to my friend here, but you will not use Gaelic. You will speak in English, so we can all enjoy your wisdom.'

'What is it you want?' said the priest.

Macleod took a chair and sat in front of him. He stared at him intently, holding back the questions, making the priest wait to understand who had come after him.

'I heard you joined the Order of Calgacus,' said Macleod.

For a moment the priest's face dropped before he caught himself. 'Order of what?'

CHAPTER 15

'The Order of Calgacus. You know. The Caledonian Warrior. I mean, I'm sure they gave you some sort of guidebook when you joined.'

'Never heard of him,' said the priest. Kirsten reached down and grabbed the man's wrist, twisting it violently. 'Ah!' cried the man.

'Don't lie,' said Kirsten. 'Just don't lie, okay? And if you are going to lie, be better than that, because you lied pretty badly. You've joined the Order of Calgacus. Why?'

The man was quiet.

'You're getting the easy side of this,' said Macleod. 'You're getting me. Some of my questions may be barbed, I may jab you a bit with the odd line, but she'll break you in two. We need answers.'

The priest looked over at Kirsten. She was giving him a smile.

'Who the hell are you people?' he said.

'Concerned citizens, something like that,' said Macleod. 'People who think that something is up. Why have you joined?'

'Right thing to do,' said the priest quietly.

'Why?'

'Our goals are aligned,' said the priest.

'What goals?' asked Macleod

'You know the Order and you don't know the goal?'

'Humour me,' said Macleod.

'No!' said the Priest.

'Well,' said Macleod 'If you're not going to bother, I'll leave you with her'

'No,' said the Priest. Kirsten stood up and was coming over. The Priest glowered at her. ' You give me the impression it's going to be bad, but it can't be that bad.'

Kirsten reached down and pulled his ear hard. The man yelled in pain.

'Shush,' she said. 'We don't want to bring people in off the street? Neither of us can cook that well.'

The man shook his head and turned away from Kirsten. But she reached down and touched somewhere on his neck. He went white, pain racing through him.

'Speak and I'll stop,' she said.

The man shook his head. 'I can't. Don't you get it? I can't.'

'Why?' asked Macleod.

'They'll come for me. If I say anything, they'll come for me. I mean, did they see you come in here? Did they?'

'Nobody knows I'm in here,' said Kirsten. 'There are a couple of people who saw me come in, but they don't know who I am. They're not dead; they're currently alive. And I'll leave, along with this gentleman, and nobody will be the wiser as to what went on.'

'Not good enough,' said the priest. 'You need to take me away; you need to get me to a sanctuary somewhere.'

'The only way you're getting out of this is by talking. Or in a box.'

The man looked over at Kirsten. 'Is that a threat?' he said.

'Of course it's a threat,' said Kirsten, 'Tell us about the Order.'

'Can you get me sanctuary?' he said. His eyes were sullen now, tears brimming.

'I can get you protection. I can get you sanctuary,' said Macleod. He looked over, and Kirsten was now behind the man, her arms raised to either side and her face inquiring *where?* Macleod ignored her.

'Where will you find me sanctuary?' asked the priest.

'I know somewhere. You can trust me or you can go out of

CHAPTER 15

here in a box,' said Macleod. 'I think that was the offer she's giving you.'

'But you can call her off, can't you?' said the man.

'No,' he said. 'She has her orders. I have mine. She's following hers; I'm executing mine. Look, there's a plot afoot, okay? And a tourist was killed because of it. But a plot against who?'

'I don't know yet. I just know we want the order to rise. It has been rising. And we still want to rise and keep going.'

'They've taken a friend of ours. Susan Cunningham. Detective from Scotland.'

'Don't know anything about that.'

'She was with Superintendent Matteo Lombardi' said Macleod. 'Do you know him? Do they have him?'

'Where do they have him?' spat Kirsten.

'I don't know,' he said. 'I truly don't know. My role is more political rather than dealing with physical obstructions. I'm in it because of my status, because of the—'

Macleod saw Kirsten looking at the window of the restaurant. It was frosted over, but right at the corner was a little chip. The frosting didn't cover well there, and seemed almost to have gone. Macleod saw Kirsten's face, and then he saw her dive to one side. Macleod threw himself down as well, as he heard the glass shatter.

The priest in front of them tipped back in the seat, the blood spattering from his face. Macleod hit the floor, rolled to one side away from the window, but then he ran over towards the dead priest.

'We need to go,' said Kirsten. 'Now!'

'He might have something on him,' said Macleod. He was looking at the deceased priest. There was just a grim face, a frightened face, but it was motionless, and Macleod couldn't look at the mess on his forehead. Instead, his hands were roaming, looking inside his cassock and coat.

'No time,' said Kirsten, and crawled from under the window over to Macleod and grabbed him.

Macleod turned from her to go out the front door.

'No,' she said. 'This way!'

Macleod was pushed through the door at the back of the restaurant, then shoved up some stairs, to a second-floor window, where he clambered onto a gantry. From there, Kirsten dragged Macleod along to the edge of the gantry and she quickly jumped up onto the railing. She turned and grabbed his hand. He was looking at her, wondering what they would do next.

'Trust me!'

He didn't have a choice. She took his hand in hers and she jumped off the gantry. Macleod didn't have time to look down. His heart pounded. He thought this could be it until he felt the cardboard boxes underneath him cushioning their fall.

Kirsten pulled him up out of them, hauling him off into an alleyway. Then he heard that universal sound of police cars arriving. Macleod and Kirsten disappeared off into the night.

Chapter 16

'How did they see us?' asked Kirsten. She stormed across the room and kicked the chair. 'How? Nobody's tailed us there.'

Macleod plodded in behind her. He sat down in the chair and let out a slow breath.

'That was a good lead. He was ready to break as well, ready to come with us. He was ready to be stashed away,' said Kirsten.

'He couldn't have been that deep in though,' said Macleod. 'Why would you have somebody like that? Somebody who broke so easily. Somebody who's—'

'It's because he's coerced into it,' said Kirsten. 'This happens a lot. He's not sold on the cult of Calgacus, or the Order, or whatever they call themselves,' she said. 'But he's in a place that they need. So they come round and they cajole him, and they say they can put him up there. And then he says yes, and then suddenly he realises what they are.'

'And what are they?' asked Macleod.

'They shot him dead without hesitation. You arrive on the scene, and they were looking to kill you too. Fanatics springs to mind,' said Kirsten. 'Cult might be the right term. People who think they can control things, who think they're above it. People who try to manipulate and then cover their tracks. We had a link in and they're gone now. More than that, they'll realise that we're on to them. They may even have seen us. They may have been watching.'

'You hauled us out by the most strange route,' said Macleod. 'That was quick thinking.'

'No, it wasn't. It was planning,' said Kirsten, turning to him suddenly. 'This is what you're not getting. The bit where you question them, the bit where you find out what's going on, that's the detection bit. That's your world, Seoras. That's what you're good at.

'The bit where I cover my backside by pre-planning and checking out the building and knowing I can get up there. The bit where I jump on a load of cardboard boxes and head off out the door, that's my world. You're used to going in with all the power. I'm used to going in with nothing.'

'And you did it well,' said Macleod. 'Twice I wouldn't be here if it wasn't for you.'

'You're damn right,' said Kirsten.

'And you came haring over here. If it hadn't been my former constable, DC Stewart, I'd be like the priest,' said Macleod.

'At least you had the wit to contact me,' said Kirsten.

'What's the matter?' asked Macleod. 'You're spitting at me as if I've done something wrong. I've come for my officer. Now you might think that I've done it recklessly, but if I'd have gone through the channels, she'd be dead.'

'She could be dead anyway,' said Kirsten. And then she spotted his face.

'Let's say she's not for the moment,' said Macleod. 'I can't think of her as dead.'

'Well, there's a chance. It's a good chance. And I know you're

CHAPTER 16

doing it for the right reasons.'

So why do I feel that you're somehow annoyed with me? Even pissed, as you would say?'

'I was out, Seoras. Do you get that? I was out. Gone. Gone from the Service. I went through hell with it. I know you sit and think that you put me up to be part of this wonderful Service, to be part of defending the UK. You put me on the track to have something bigger and better than what I was. See next time? Don't! You see somebody else like that? Bump them up the police force. Don't send them into this world.'

'Why?' asked Macleod.

'Craig turned on us. Craig!'

'I know he had his problems. I know—'

'You don't get it. We had to put him down! Well, you don't want to know about that.'

'Not Anna.'

'No, we didn't put down Anna. We is Anna and me. The whole damn thing imploded, Seoras. People we worked with. Close people. Yeah, I left, okay. I was in Brazil, South America. I was out and just getting on with it. With life.'

'You gave me the phone,' said Macleod suddenly. 'You answered it. Kirsten, you came.'

'Because I owe you.'

'No, not because you owe me,' said Macleod. 'Because you know it's the right thing to do. You know me and you know I'm not here because of some ego trip or because of some sort of pride. I'm here to get a damn good constable back. You know that.'

'Yeah,' she said. 'And I was out, dammit. Out of this.'

'Well, get your head back in it. We need to get her.'

'But we've got a dead end,' Kirsten said. 'A completely dead end. Is there anything else you can pull out of Matteo's notes? Anybody else we can go after? I didn't see anything. I suppose we could send it off to get somebody who reads Italian well to dig out something else and—'

Macleod put his hand up. 'Hold it,' he said. 'Wait a second.' He dug into the pockets of his coat and produced what looked like rubbish.

'What's that?' asked Kirsten.

'While you were pulling me off him,' said Macleod, 'my hands went through the priest's pockets. I didn't have time to check what was in them. I just stuffed it into mine. Let's see what we've got.'

He put the pocket debris on the table in front of him and started separating it out. There were a set of pocket matches, a flyer for the theatre, a restaurant card, and a receipt from the cafe.

'Get a map up. You're better at that sort of thing,' he said. 'I want to know where all these places are.'

Kirsten sat down with her phone and inputted the name of the café, the name on the pocket matches, the theatre and also the restaurant card.

'Well, it's a bit of a mishmash,' she said, 'the theatre's very far away.'

'It's a flyer,' said Macleod, 'it might not have come from the theatre itself.'

'The pocket matches are from . . . it's actually a nightclub. Would you believe it? Don't know what he was doing there. The restaurant and the café, however, are very close to it.'

'Therefore, he's been there fairly recently. As for the rest of it, the restaurant, he might have been to recently, as he's got the card for it. Thought it was good. Might go back. Receipt

CHAPTER 16

from the cafe. Clearly shows he was there yesterday. Pocket matches. The nightclub. He was a smoker,' said Macleod.

'What?' asked Kirsten.

'He was a smoker. Did you see his fingers? Yellow. Could also smell smoke off the coat. Not off the cassock.'

Kirsten stared at him.

'You wanted the detective. The detective is here. And when did you lose that ability?'

'It all gets a little more blood and thunder, what I do,' she said.

'He was dead,' said Macleod. 'The only evidence he was going to give you was on him. We needed to check it out.'

'We needed to get the hell out. Somebody had just shot him dead,' said Kirsten.

'Still,' said Macleod, 'we got a place to go to. Why was he in this area yesterday?'

'It's a bit of a long shot. Could have nothing to do with Susan.'

'It could have everything to do with her,' said Macleod. 'He said he had already heard the tale, about someone being gone after. How'd he know that?

'Could have told him to put some fear into him.'

'No. No,' said Macleod, 'you wouldn't. Would you? If he'd have nothing to do with it, if he had nothing to do with that purpose, why would he know? If he's just a puppet on the outside, he wouldn't know.

'Well then, I guess we go have a look. We'll go in the morning,' said Kirsten. 'Early morning.'

'Why not now?' asked Macleod.

'They'll lock up tight. They'll be worried about people coming to see. The thing is,' said Kirsten, 'they'll get to hear of

Conti's death. If they do, the best thing they can do is bed down. Did Conti say where anybody was? You don't immediately start racing around and trying to take someone to task. The activity dies until they find out what happened. They may also know that Conti didn't say anything. After all, they shot him quickly. He must have had a double-tail.'

'A what?' said Macleod.

'A double-tail. He arrived, went in. You followed him in. Somebody else was still watching.'

'I didn't see anyone,' said Macleod.

'Well, you wouldn't, would you? You're not skilled enough for that.'

Macleod gave a sigh. 'Could have told me to look for him.'

'No,' said Kirsten, 'because if you look for it in such an amateur fashion, they'll know what you are. They'll know what I am. Not just interested parties.'

'Well, you're the boss,' said Macleod, 'so what do we do?'

'First thing tomorrow morning,' said Kirsten; 'get some sleep. You're going back into the old Italian clothes as well. We're going to be on the street.'

The next morning, Kirsten and Macleod walked out to the area that had been indicated from the map on the phone. They identified the cafe, the restaurant, and the nightclub where the matches came from. They made their way to a cafe for breakfast. As they sat there, they watched what seemed like normal life in Rome. People on the go, ready to head off to work, grabbing an early breakfast and their coffee. But Kirsten was peering past this daily minutiae to see what was going on.

'Who are the people who are always here?' she asked.

'What do you mean?' retorted Macleod.

'When you're normally looking for people, the bad guys

CHAPTER 16

will hide. The people who are contacts, the people who are patrolling the areas, will also hide in plain sight,' said Kirsten. 'Take that newspaper seller over there.'

There was a small stall with a man sat in it, smoking. He grunted every now and again when someone came past, but most would take a paper and just throw some change at him. His feet were up on the side of the stall, and there was a radio in the background, playing some sort of chat station. Macleod couldn't make out what they were saying.

'Do you think he's worth grabbing then, do you?'

'No,' said Kirsten. 'He's the watchman. He's the man they come to and they pass messages through, and he passes the messages back out. What we need to watch for is the person who goes to him the most often. We've got a full day ahead of us, Seoras,' she said.

The rest of the day was spent at different parts of the street and watching what was going on. They didn't do it together, parting occasionally to take a few hours out of the way. Kirsten also gave Macleod a lesson on how to change his appearance, so he didn't look as if he'd kept returning.

When they gathered together to explain what they'd seen, they found several men going back and forward to the newspaper stand. Together they returned, standing down the street from the newspaper stand seller and spotted one man that they'd both identified.

'So, what do we do now?' asked Macleod.

'Go down that alleyway over there,' Kirsten told Macleod. 'Wait for me.'

Macleod did as instructed and was standing in the alleyway for several minutes. He wondered where she'd gone. From around the corner, into the deeper recesses of the alleyway,

Kirsten came, almost carrying a man.

She threw him up against the wall, a hand across his mouth and a forearm against his throat. Macleod could see he was struggling to breathe, but he also saw that Kirsten was strong enough that the forearm was holding the man up just off the ground as well. She let her hand across his mouth come away and she watched the man incredibly carefully.

'Who are you working for?' asked Kirsten.

'No,' said the man.

'I know you speak English.' Kirsten punched him in the stomach, dragging even more breath out of him. 'I know you speak English very well. Who are you working for?'

The man went to shake his head. Macleod saw Kirsten force the forearm even harder into the man's throat. There was almost a whisper. 'Conti.'

'And what do you do for Conti?' asked Kirsten, releasing the pressure with her forearm ever so slightly.

'I know nothing,' he said. 'I'm the message man. Just pass messages.'

'And where has Father Conti been round here,' asked Macleod, 'that he needs messages?'

The man shook his head, but Kirsten leaned in hard again.

'You have five seconds,' she said, 'or I will break your throat. You will die. Five. Four. Three.'

The man's hand went up. He pointed out of the alleyway and up. 'Flat,' he said.

Kirsten released his throat and the man's feet landed on the ground, but by the time he'd realised this, she'd smacked him. She broke his nose, and he collapsed to the ground, out cold. She reached inside her jacket and tied the man up with the several bits of rope she had.

CHAPTER 16

'Keep an eye on that flat,' she said. 'I'm just going to get rid of him and clean up a bit.' She saw Macleod's horrified look.

'He's a nasty piece of work, and he's not dead,' said Kirsten.

'We could just keep him tied up.'

Kirsten looked around her. 'With what police force, Seoras? We're on our own out here. It's an extraction, I told you. Watch that flat.'

It's several minutes before Macleod was joined again by Kirsten. And over his shoulder, she hummed and hawed.

'How do we get in there, Seoras?' she said. 'They'll see us come in.'

'Just go up and knock,' he said.

'We have to work out who's in there,' she said. 'So we have to work out who comes out. If Matteo is in there, and if somebody doesn't come out, they can kill him while we're at the door. There's you and there's me. Okay? And you are not racing in, because, frankly, you'd be useless. I'll be well outnumbered, possibly. I don't know. We need to recce the place to work out how we get in, who's there. We don't do this quickly.'

'And what about that man that you've just tied up?'

'What about him?' said Kirsten. 'He'll not be doing anything for a while.' Macleod gave her a look, but Kirsten remained stone-faced. 'Don't ask me. I won't tell you.'

As they stood there, Macleod could see a beggar woman climbing the steps to the flat. The front of the building had a window where you could see the stairs all the way up to the upper floors. The beggar woman was going past the second and then the third floor before she headed across to a flat, the one the man had been pointed to.

'What's up?' asked Kirsten, watching him stare.

'I don't know,' said Macleod, 'but it looks like it's worth

watching.'

Chapter 17

Macleod watched as the limping beggar woman, who was wrapped in a large shawl, approached the door of the flat. From the angle across the street, he could see through the window. As she was higher up, several floors above him, the angle didn't give him a complete view of her. However, the shawl looked like an old rug, rather than any decorative item. The woman's hair was distressed. He could see dirt or muck on the side of her face, and a bare leg beneath the shawl, leading to a bare foot.

There was a whiteness about her, though. She didn't have the Iberian tan, or that Italian richness of colour in her skin. She hobbled as she walked, but it was less of a stutter, more like she was leaning to one side.

Macleod watched as she knocked on the front door of the flat. Words were said that he couldn't hear from his position. But then she turned and walked away again, that same awkward hobble. He couldn't see her leg on this side, for the shawl was draped right down. Her hand was inside the shawl as well, but he thought he saw a faint smile across her lips as she left the door. Unusual, considering the fact no money seemed to have changed hands.

In response to her obvious need, a crowd watched as she hobbled down the stairs that led up to the flat. She came out into the street, but she didn't go far. The beggar sat down, the shawl still tight around one side of her, a single bare leg poking out. She had a cup that must have been rinsed out from one of the trendy coffee stores without its logo on the side of the paper cup. And the odd person threw some change in, but many people swore at her, or just ignored her completely.

Kirsten and Macleod continued to watch the flat above. Several men disappeared to a nearby cafe along the street where they sat drinking beer. They continued to watch as several of the men went back and then came out again.

'How many have we seen?' asked Kirsten.

'Five?' said Macleod. 'There's four of them now, having a beer.'

'So there's only one that we've seen back up in the flat.'

'That's right,' said Macleod. 'Do you think this is what they're doing?'

'Doing what?' asked Kirsten.

'All popping out for a beer. Rotating, so nobody misses out.'

'It's not proper practice,' she said. 'You'd have your beer inside; you wouldn't come out.'

'This is an order of something or other,' said Macleod. 'These are not necessarily trained professionals.'

'No,' said Kirsten. 'And here's the other thing. These guys may not even be from the Order. Maybe the Order is using them to hold Matteo. After all, if they get caught, Matteo says these are the people from the Order. Yet, they'll have no idea about any of it.'

'So you think that Father Conti was the key person?' said Macleod.

CHAPTER 17

'Could be. Could be the major link. He was running the operation to keep Matteo. And then they shot him when they thought he was going to blab.'

'Closes the loop, doesn't it?' said Macleod.

'It does, but it also means that they'll be looking to see where Matteo is.'

'So, we have to get there first,' said Macleod.

'We do,' said Kirsten, 'if Matteo's inside. I find it difficult to believe they haven't got somebody inside. After all, why not all come out together?'

'Exactly,' said Macleod. 'So how do we do this?'

'Well,' said Kirsten, 'we could just go up and storm in. It's difficult to get into that flat. There's nowhere to sneak up from outside. It's perfectly positioned. Although, I wouldn't like it. It's not easy to get out of either.'

'Look,' said Macleod, 'the beggar woman's on her feet again.'

'She's got a funny shuffle,' said Kirsten.

They watched as the woman hobbled along, leaning awkwardly, and made her way back up the steps. Together, Macleod and Kirsten strode across the street and entered the building. Macleod clocked a quick look to see if the men were still drinking at the bar. They were doing so, and he gave a sigh of relief as he tried to follow the beggar woman up the stairs.

She'd had a good start on them though, and by the time they got to the third floor, she was already heading towards the door. From behind, Macleod saw the shawl creeping down more on one side to cover a leg, except it flapped, and there was no leg there. He looked again. There was no leg. He leaned over to Kirsten.

'That's Susan Cunningham,' he whispered. 'That's who we've

come for.'

'What's she doing?' asked Kirsten. But before she could say anything further, the door of the flat opened.

Everything happened at once in Macleod mind. The door opened and the one man they had clocked but who hadn't gone to the bar emerged. Beside him, Macleod heard Kirsten mutter under her breath.

'Four at the bar, one from inside. All five. They're protecting no one.'

He was going to ask her what she meant except she took off at speed. By the time the door was fully opened and the man was standing outside, Kirsten had reached the door at speed behind the beggar woman. With a swing of the left arm, she knocked the beggar to one side, barrelling herself into the man at the front door.

The beggar lady cried out as she bounced over to the side wall and Macleod ran towards her. Meanwhile, Kirsten was trying to get to her feet. The man she clattered into had gone straight down, but Kirsten had followed through and rolled inside the flat.

Macleod reached down to the beggar woman, who turned around and looked into his eyes.

'Seoras,' she said. 'You came.'

'On your feet,' he said, and suddenly caught himself. 'Sorry, on your—'

'Just go,' she shouted, grabbing his hand and allowing him to pull her up onto her good leg. The shawl was dropped to one side. The arm previously covered was revealed to be holding onto a crutch, and together they raced towards the stairs. From behind them somebody shouted in Italian, something Macleod couldn't make out. Susan Cunningham understood it meant

CHAPTER 17

'Halt. I have a gun.'

Susan turned, and Macleod looked as well to see a man holding a gun towards them. However, what the man didn't see was behind him. A figure reached round with her arm and casually snapped his neck. Macleod felt a horror as Kirsten Stewart stepped over the man and kicked the fallen gun away.

Macleod turned round, arm helping to support Susan, and they reached the stairs to go down. However, they saw four men coming up; the four from the pub. Had they phoned through? Had they contacted their man?

'Get in the lift,' said Kirsten under her breath as she approached them. 'Go up, not down. Back way out. Find somewhere. Find an escape. Don't come back for me,' said Kirsten.

Macleod gave her a look of 'are you sure?' but he could see there was a wildness in her eyes. He wrapped his arm around Susan Cunningham and headed towards the lift, pressing the button. As he turned back, he saw the first man approach the landing on the third floor. For his trouble, he received a left hand straight to the jaw, sending him tumbling back down the stairs.

His fall slowed down one man coming up, but another two approached Kirsten Stewart. One delivered a blow to her shoulder while the other caught the back of her hand. She spun as she grabbed the third man's arm, sending him across the landing. But the man who'd been delayed, dived forward, grabbing her legs. Kirsten still stood upright, but was fighting to stay that way.

The other men had rallied back up, and Macleod saw that there were two approaching Kirsten. She caught one with an arm around the head, holding him tight, while her left arm prodded out, poking the other one in the eyes. The one she'd grabbed round the head, she twisted, causing him to stumble away, and then drove her elbow down the top of the one who'd grabbed her legs.

'Get in the damn lift, Seoras!' she shouted. The lift doors had just opened and Macleod felt himself being dragged in by Susan Cunningham.

As the door closed, he saw Kirsten take a blow to the face and reel, standing up to face three attackers. At least one had a knife out. He couldn't do this, couldn't just let her take them on. He needed to help.

As he reached for the button, Susan put her hand across.

'No, she told you to go,' she said.

'I need to help her. You go up,' he said.

'Let's be honest,' said Susan, 'I'd be more help to her than you would.'

Macleod looked at her, standing there with a crutch, half her leg gone, but he knew she was right. The door closed, and they were taken away from the world of pain outside. They got to the tenth floor, stepped out onto the landing, and Macleod looked around.

'Which one's the fire escape?' he said. 'None of it's in English.'

'They do have pictures like we do,' said Susan. She swung her way over to the wall to look at the fire diagram on the wall. As she reached it, they heard a gunshot. It was from below them, well below them, and Macleod's heart pounded.

'I need to help her,' he said.

'You can't,' said Susan. 'Down here. We need to go.'

Macleod turned back. He would get the lift back down, get to the third floor and help her. He would . . .

CHAPTER 17

'If they hit her with a shot, she's gone,' said Susan. 'These people, they don't mess about. They're not...'

'Not what?' asked Macleod.

'Not normal criminals.'

He could feel his hands beginning to tighten. His palms going sweaty. It wasn't just anybody down there. It was Kirsten. Kirsten was someone he'd taken an interest in. Someone he'd been through cases with. Someone who had rescued him the other day from almost certain death and he was abandoning her. He couldn't do that. Susan Cunningham grabbed his arm.

'She told you to get me out of here. I know what's going on. You go back down, this all ends. I need to get away. I need to tell you what's happening.'

Macleod nodded. He fought back tears, wondering what would happen to Kirsten. Another shot rang out.

Susan Cunningham pushed open the door to see stairs descending. Macleod was amazed at how she fought her way down them. One leg, one crutch, working them, almost as if the crutch was part of her. He stumbled down behind her, all ten floors, and when he hit the bottom, he was out of breath. But Susan looked fit, like she could climb up again.

'Hit that door for me,' she said.

Macleod reached forward, pushed the door into the sunshine outside. He stumbled into an alleyway.

'Where do we go?' he said.

Susan looked up. She could hear sirens. She turned right. 'This will take us into the alleyway at the back,' she said. 'We don't want to go in the street. I'm a bit of a giveaway.'

Together, they raced as hard as they could. Reaching the end of the alleyway, they looked left and right, down another tight section. There was a laundry at the far end. They could see the steam and sheets being taken in and out, loading up into a van.

'Down that way,' said Macleod. 'They can't bring a car from in front of us. They can only come from behind. If we get past that van, they can't follow.'

'They can't get a car down here at all,' said Susan.

She hopped along, almost outpacing Macleod. As they reached the laundry van, there were cries and shrieks. Maybe the gunshots had been heard, because the wheeled baskets had laundry in them, but nobody near them. Had everyone run inside? Was everyone hiding? The sirens sounded like they were behind them on the road. They raced forward again, past the laundry van.

'This is going to bring us out on the street,' said Susan, 'we don't want to do that.'

'Those sirens are behind us,' said Macleod. 'We can't go there. Do we just jump in a taxi,' he said.

'Of course not, they're looking for a woman with a crutch and one leg,' she said. 'The police are looking for me. I'm kind of a giveaway at the moment. We need to get out of here, we need to get—'

A car pulled up at the edge of the alleyway out by the street. The windows were tinted. It looked sporty. Nothing too flashy, but like a car someone with a reasonably modest bank account might buy to be more impressive. The passenger side window rolled down.

Macleod looked forward, peering into the inside of the car.

'Move it!' came a shout from inside. Susan grabbed Macleod's arm.

'Go!' she said. 'Go!'

CHAPTER 17

As they reached the car, Macleod threw open the front door and jumped into the passenger seat. Behind him, Susan opened the rear door, throwing her crutch in and then dumping herself inside, pulling the door shut behind her. The passenger side window rolled up automatically, and before Macleod had even closed the door, the car was pulling away.

Macleod turned to look at Kirsten Stewart driving. The side of her face was covered in blood.

'Are you all right?' he said.

'Do I flippin' look all right, Seoras.'

'Where do we go?' he said.

'We go back to our base. I'll drop you two very close. Get in, lock up, and wait for me.'

'Are you sure you'll make it back?' he said. 'You're bleeding a lot.'

'Just do as you're told. My job, my business,' said Kirsten.

The car raced away, and then slowed somewhat, driving quite modestly through Rome. Clearly, Kirsten wasn't wanting to pick up any attention. Macleod turned round in his seat and looked at Susan Cunningham, lying across the seats in the back. She gave a huge smile.

'It's good to see you,' she said. 'You got my message, apparently.' It was all Macleod could do to stop the tears from filling his eyes.

Chapter 18

'Are you okay? Can I give you any help?'

'It's fine,' said Kirsten. 'It looks a lot worse than it is.'

'It certainly looks bad,' said Susan. 'Are you sure I can't help?'

'Just take a seat. Seoras is going to want to talk to you. I'll be through in a minute. I just need to get cleaned and patched up. In fact, can you bring me the small box I left on the side of the living room?'

Susan Cunningham swung herself back out of the bathroom, grabbed the box with one hand in the living room and then swung herself back over to the bathroom. Susan fought to stop herself from gasping at some gashes that had opened up in Kirsten's skin.

'What's in the box?'

'Stuff to fix myself,' she said. 'Painkillers and ointment to sort out the wounds, antiseptics, the lot. In my job, sometimes you don't get a doctor, so you've got to learn to look after yourself.'

Kirsten's hair was tied up in a ponytail behind her head, and Susan could see the bruising on her neck.

'Are you the one who used to work for him?'

CHAPTER 18

'Why do you say that?' asked Kirsten.

'Seoras. Few people call him Seoras. They'd have to be a good friend or in his team. Even then he still gets "Sir." Hope always talks about Kirsten. Used to work with the team. Kirsten went off to the Service. And well, I'm kind of deep in trouble at the moment. Makes sense he would reach out to someone within the Service.'

'I'm not service anymore,' said Kirsten. 'I don't do that. But I came here because he said you were in trouble. I came here to help him. He's a daft old bugger sometimes. He should have just told me what to do. Where to find you. I'd have come and got you. But he had to come here too. He had to make sure you were all right.'

'And so, what now?' asked Susan as Kirsten continued to wipe down the side of her face.

'What now? My thoughts are I get you out of here. And him. Clear out.'

'But Matteo's still in trouble. Matteo helped me. He—'

'Well . . .'

'He's the one who really understands what's behind all this. He's the—'

'Save it for now,' said Kirsten. 'I'll be done soon. And I'll sit down and you can tell us all you know. If needs be, I'll get to him. But we'll get you two out of here.'

Susan nodded and swung her way back into the living room; Macleod appeared and sat down on the sofa beside her.

'You okay?' he asked. He had a smile on his face that rarely got so large.

'I'm good,' said Susan. 'A little shaken up, but I'm good.'

'I'll get some coffee on,' said Macleod, standing up.

'I can do it,' said Susan.

'No, you sit. You're about to get grilled.'

'Grilled?' said Susan.

'I need to understand what's going on. I need to work out the best next move. To do that, I'm going to have to get out of you everything you know, even if you don't know you know it.'

'I was hoping it would be a little more friendly than that.'

'It'll be friendly,' said Macleod. 'But what you're involved in here, it's big.'

'I got that feeling.'

'Big enough that they ran a trap to get hold of us. A trap to pull you in. I need to work out why you were there.'

'Okay,' said Susan.

She watched as the older man got up and walked into the kitchen to make coffee. He came back with three mugs, all black, and put two down in front of the sofa and left the third beside an armchair. A few minutes later, Kirsten Stewart walked back in. Her hair was untied now, presumably to cover the bruising on her neck. She had a smile on her face, but it was one that Susan didn't trust. There was definitely an anxiousness about the woman.

'So what happened?' asked Macleod. 'Take us through it.'

'Well,' said Susan. 'It was all fine. I rang you and explained it as such. But Matteo—or rather, Superintendent Lombardi—he was . . . well, he was very kind. But I got the feeling it was because he wanted to offload something.'

'Where did you meet him?' asked Kirsten.

'When we arrived at the airport. He was there.'

'And he definitely works for the police.'

'His boss is Ricci. And yes, definitely worked there. We went into the building. Met his boss, everyone.'

CHAPTER 18

'You were here to investigate a murder?'

'A suspicious death,' said Susan. 'They wanted some help from our side. Ricci kept pushing that it was accidental. But it didn't look like it. And Lombardi had ideas it wasn't. We followed these through. We found that Hamish Ferguson, the man in question, had moved bedroom in his accommodation. The police hadn't realised this.

'We got to search his original room and there were detailed notes about what he was doing over here.'

'Which was,' asked Kirsten.

'He was a genealogist following up from the Order of Calgacus, or Calgacus at least. He was a Caledonian fighter against the Romans, got defeated. But Hamish could trace his origins back to him and traced them over here, with a few other survivors. He discovered there was an order of Calgacus, people who could trace their own lineage back operating what he at first thought was a social club. Alas not.

'He was to meet with them and then he died. The fall he had seemed strange, but they couldn't pin it on anyone. Would have been tough to though. Somebody could have pushed him off and you wouldn't know.

'So what happened after that?' asked Macleod.

'Well, we followed the evidence. We found where he had been. Toured around, realised he'd been to the baths of Diocletian. When we went there, we found the guide was annoyed because there had been a meeting, and they had got no overtime. We used CCTV footage to show that the meeting had many well-known people at it.

'I suggested taking it to Ricci, but Matteo didn't want to. That's when he opened up. Said he thought Ricci was not who he said he was, or maybe involved. There was some paper found, giving a location and a time. It was on a street in Rome, among the poor areas. The time for the meeting was that day, so Matteo and I went to seek it out. That's where it all went wrong.

'We got into the building where the meeting was taking place, and we overheard their plans, well, their talk of a significant event. You could tell something was up, because they said nothing plainly. Everything was done in code, or cryptically, in case they were overheard. But it was a significant event, and they talked about taking over the top job in the country.'

'What, like the presidency?'

'No, Kirsten,' said Susan. 'Matteo said to me he believed that someone had been quietly taking on individuals to move people within the order of Calgacus up the ranks. Get them higher into political and church fields. He said there was possibly an attempt on the Prime Minister. That's what he believed this was.

'As we were getting out, well, that's where it went wrong. We were seen. Chased in the area. Matteo cut off down one way. There were several of them with him. He knew I wouldn't outrun them. I can get about on this crutch but not like that. Believing he was caught, I went underground and did the beggar trick.'

'You did it well,' said Macleod. 'It took me a while to recognise it was you there.' Kirsten didn't even clock your stick.

'You mean the crutch? I spent a lot of time in the street picking up on rumours and whispers. I found out that Father Conti was probably involved. He visited the area, and he'd been part of the meeting as well. I did what I could to follow him. It wasn't easy, but he seemed to come out towards that area the flat was in. So, I spent time there and could soon spot that something was up in that flat. Same people. The four of them then were out, so I thought that was my chance. There were only five of them there.'

'Conti was a dummy. Somebody else has him,' said Kirsten. 'It's a dummy cover-up. They put it out there and they make sure it gets noticed. They make it reasonably high profile. I should have seen it,' she said. 'I should have seen it.'

'You can't blame yourself,' said Macleod.

'I can and I will, Seoras. I should have seen it. This is my world. It's what I operate in. Don't have the luxury of barging in, getting it wrong, and then barging in somewhere else. I don't have all the backup. Need to check it thoroughly before you do it. Shouldn't have had you two there either.'

'Let's save the recriminations for another time,' said Macleod. He turned back to Susan. 'But you also got that message out, didn't you?'

'It was tough,' said Susan. 'I dropped my phone as well while escaping. So I went to the library, sent an SMS text message, but you haven't got my number.'

'Your private number,' said Macleod.

'Hope does. So that's why I sent it to Hope.'

'I received many text messages telling me you were off for a week's leave, looking for a leave of absence. Ricci even phoned up to confirm it,' said Macleod.

'So Ricci's definitely involved,' said Kirsten.

'And if he's involved, well then,' said Macleod, 'this has got police corruption written all over it.'

'It's more high level than that,' said Kirsten. 'If they're talking about putting people up in different professions, they'll have people in each of them. People who are compromised. Church as well. Look at Conti.'

'I'm impressed,' said Macleod. 'You survived out here.'

'Unlike you. He turned up, blundered in, nearly got himself killed and had to be hauled out,' said Kirsten. 'We then followed some leads and ended up after Conti. We got duped into that as well. I guess it was lucky for all of us we ended up in the same place together.'

'Doesn't seem to be that lucky for you,' said Susan.

'I've had worse,' said Kirsten. Susan pulled a face like she didn't believe it.

'She's had worse,' said Macleod quietly. 'Don't ask.'

'So what do we do with this, then? You're here now. Told you what I know, but I have got no evidence. Nothing firm. Matteo had it all.'

'We've been to Matteo's house,' said Kirsten. 'What we've pulled out is certainly not enough evidence, just suspicion. So, if there's hard evidence, he must have hidden it elsewhere. Because this stuff was hidden well within the house.'

'But you will not keep the good stuff in your house,' said Macleod, 'will you? It's going to be elsewhere. We need to find Matteo.'

'The thing you need to understand is,' said Susan, 'we have got little time.'

'You have got no time at all,' said Kirsten. 'You two are out of here.'

'What do you mean?' asked Macleod.

'Extraction. That's what I signed up for. She's here. I'll get you over the border, I'll get you back to the UK. And you two are done. I'll take it on then. Notify who needs to be notified. There are contacts within the national Services. I'll find out who's legit. I'll pass it on and let the Italians deal with it.'

CHAPTER 18

'How long's that going to take? asked Susan.

'A couple of weeks to get things moving. I need to do it on the quiet. Make sure I'm not involved with it. So, I can disappear again.'

'That's not going to work,' said Susan. 'You see, the significant event they were talking about, to take over the top job, it's in two days' time.'

'What?' blurted Macleod.

'It's in two days' time. Matteo has the evidence. Matteo can link you in. If we have the evidence, you can go to the right people with the evidence.'

'What if we don't?' said Macleod. 'How do we play it then?'

Kirsten stood up and paced. 'If we had that evidence, we could dump it in front of someone. I could just take it to the Service, the Italian Service, put it in front of them. I could even take it to Anna and leave it with her.'

'Who the heck's Anna?' asked Susan.

'Anna Hunt,' said Macleod. 'She's high in the Service, the British service.'

'She is the Service,' said Kirsten absentmindedly, which caused Macleod to look at her bemusedly. Kirsten shook her head. 'Whatever we do is going to be too slow,' she said. 'We need Matteo. We need to find out who these people are, the evidence he's got against him, and then we connect. Until we get that, I won't be able to get Anna to act over here.'

'But somebody's going to die,' said Susan.

'Some Italian is going to die,' said Kirsten. 'Anna Hunt will not create an international incident—using her people, working underneath and without jurisdiction—to prevent the death of one Italian.'

'But it could be somebody important.'

'They're all important,' said Macleod.

'It won't matter,' said Kirsten. 'Matteo. We need to sit down and work out how to get Matteo.'

'What if he's dead?' asked Macleod.

'Then we need to get his evidence. The evidence is the important thing, not Matteo.'

'Not sure I agree with you,' said Susan.

'Sorry,' said Kirsten. 'I know what to do. It sounds cold, but you focus on what the important bit is, and that is the important bit, because the job doesn't get done without it. If Matteo's dead, he's dead.'

'No,' said Susan. 'We need to get him.'

Kirsten almost shook her head. But she turned away, looking over to the far wall, as if needing inspiration. 'Two days,' said Kirsten. 'We need to work out how, and we need to get on with it. It looks like you two aren't going home yet.'

Chapter 19

'It has to be Ricci,' said Macleod. 'He's the one tangible lead we've got. We know he's involved.'

'We don't know how or if he's even a big part or a small part of it,' said Kirsten.

'He spoke to me on the phone,' said Macleod. 'He was the one who put the lie out. He must have taken the phone and sent the text message over, pretending it was from Susan, saying she was away for the week looking for leave.'

'You don't know that. He may just be a pawn and be used. Seoras, you've got to explore every avenue. You've got to widen out your thought process. If we get this wrong, we're in trouble.'

'In two days, we're in trouble anyway,' said Susan.

'We're not. Somebody else is. We have to watch our own back with this,' said Kirsten.

'We need Matteo. We need to save him. Getting to Ricci will help us do that,' said Susan.

'We kind of agree on that one,' said Macleod. 'If he's his boss in the force, they're more likely to have used him to watch Matteo. If Ricci's still even on the go. They may have despatched him. If Ricci was watching Matteo closely, he shouldn't have got that close to the Order. At the end of the day,' said Macleod, 'he's the only one, okay?'

'Fine,' said Kirsten. 'But I go. You both stay here. Seoras, we're in Italy. You don't speak Italian, don't know the customs, and don't know their ways.'

'I do,' said Susan. 'With all due respect, I kept myself hidden.'

'With all due respect, you've only had one disguise. As a beggar. What happens when you need to get into places? If you have to, you're a dead giveaway,' said Kirsten. 'I'm sorry. I don't mean to be ableist, but with your leg the way it is at the moment, you stand out like a sore thumb.'

'So what? We just sit here?' asked Susan.

'That's it, I'll go. See what he's up to. Check what's happening with him. You two, in the meantime, try to come up with something else. Sit and talk; sit and work out if there's anything else that's in that head,' said Kirsten, pointing at Susan Cunningham.

'If there's nothing else,' said Kirsten, 'I'll get on to Ricci. It'll probably take me a few hours at least. The problem is, during the day, he's going to be doing his job. If he's going to be doing anything else, it's liable to happen at night. But I'll tail him. Give me the details of the building, where he is. Run me through what he looks like, Susan. Run me through anything else you know about him, car, clothing, whatever.'

Susan sat down with Kirsten, giving out the details while Macleod went through and washed coffee cups in the sink. After a while, Kirsten came through.

'This is not how I work,' said Macleod. 'I need to be you.'

'What, in charge? You're never in charge in my work,' said Kirsten, 'and that's why you wouldn't work in the Service. I never know everything, never understand everything. I've got to be thinking four or five steps ahead, looking all around me for anything that's coming. You're used to being the authority, the one that's allowed to investigate. I've spent the last few years being somebody else.'

'I missed you on the team. You know that?' said Macleod. 'For all the others that have come along, I've missed you. You were closest to thinking like me.'

'I still do think like you.'

'I don't think so,' said Macleod. 'You gun people down, yes, to save me, I get it,' said Macleod, 'but I don't think I could bring myself to do that.'

'I do what's necessary when it's necessary,' said Kirsten. 'I decide and I do it. That guy was going to kill you. Some of the others up at the flat would have killed me. I don't just kill recklessly.'

'Look,' said Macleod, 'don't shut me out, okay? I know you think this is your world, and great, but don't lock me out. This is corruption in the police force.'

'This is bigger than that,' said Kirsten. 'And I'm not shutting you out. I'm teaching you how to operate in this environment. You used to teach me, remember? You're out of your depth here, Seoras. Trust me. I know you mean well. And I love you came for her, that you care that much. But you should have flagged it and stayed away.'

'Take care of yourself out there,' he said. 'Okay?'

'I always do. And you won't just be sitting here on your bottom. I don't know what's going on yet but once I see Ricci up to something, you'll be involved. Two days is not long enough but I can't afford slip-ups. You're an old man, Seoras. You haven't got the fitness to run around.'

'You'd rather I'd sent—'

'No. Yes, she could fight better than you. But you and I think on the same lines. I understand you see someone in trouble. We want to stop them. We want to save that person. But this is bigger. Sometimes you've got to think when to step away. Hope would have run off to the authorities by now. Hope wouldn't see the big picture this way. She'd look for a simple and neat way out of it, but it isn't here. You know I'm glad it's you,' said Kirsten.

Macleod stepped forward, and together they hugged. 'I wish I'd kept you with us,' said Macleod. 'I wish I hadn't sent you away.'

'Why? Because you're not happy with what I've become?'

'You're not happy you've had to become it?'

'Don't worry,' said Kirsten. 'Despite all the pain and all the close shaves, I'll be finding my feet again. I'll be back up and at it.'

'Just watch yourself out there.'

'I'll be in touch. Give her the earpiece.'

'The what?' asked Macleod. 'Earpiece. You've got one. In the box over there, there's another one. Show her how to put it in her ear and pop it on. Okay?'

'Will it have a transmit thing? Will I be able to talk to her and her to me?'

'Just keep it simple, you're not ready for full comms yet.'

Kirsten left the building, leaving Macleod and Susan Cunningham to sit and go over what had happened again. Kirsten was restless, though. It was with a practiced ease that she identified Ricci and watched what he was doing in the station throughout the day. Using headscarves because she couldn't tie her hair up, Kirsten kept changing her look and kept changing clothes.

CHAPTER 19

She was able to monitor the inspector throughout his day. However, it was strictly police business. In the evening, however, he disappeared out in his own in a car, and Kirsten followed him, in one she had stolen. Another reason she didn't want Macleod to come along was he got annoyed at this petty theft. She did it because it was necessary.

Going to hire a car from someone just left traces. Picking one up every day—well, that was just easier.

Ricci arrived at dinner to meet a sassy black-haired woman. She was clearly in her fifties, but she had a look of class about her. She also had curves and stature, something that annoyed Kirsten.

Kirsten, for all that she was—a fighter, a woman with strength, defined muscles, silky black hair, and tenacity to boot—was not a woman a lot of men desired. She was too full on with her fighting side. She didn't have that dress sense that poured over sexuality. Instead, Kirsten was more practical.

If you liked the look of the hiking boots, well, she was maybe your girl. But this woman was all class. Necklaces, earrings, the hair swept around and the dress that dared to say, 'You'll love what's underneath.'

Ricci seemed to be getting on fine with her. They had wine with their meal, an expensive looking one at that. Kirsten called Macleod, telling him to get out here with Susan Cunningham. She detailed to them the route to travel, where to walk where they would be least seen. She picked them up in the park that was just beside the restaurant, in darkness, under some trees. The three of them sat watching the window of the restaurant.

'You got me out for what' asked Macleod. 'He's sitting having a romantic meal. Who's the woman?'

'I don't know,' said Kirsten. 'I don't think he's phoned anyone all day and she, well . . . I'm not sure this is a date.'

'How come?' asked Macleod. 'Look at her, she's set up to be a date. He's nice and smart, and they're having food.'

'It's not a date,' said Susan; 'look at them.'

Macleod watched closely. It wasn't, was it. They didn't have that hunger for each other. Some words that were being spoken, even though they were in Italian, seemed to be too crisp, too quick. It wasn't playful. There were serious transactions going on.

'Can you lip-read?' Macleod said to Susan.

'Are you for real?' she said. 'I speak Italian a little, but good enough, you know, I get by. I can't lip-read it.'

'Can you do it, Kirsten?'

'No,' said Kirsten. 'I can lip-read English perfectly, but not this.'

'Oh, well then, we won't know what's going on unless we get closer.'

'They've just finished the pudding. I think they'll be on the move,' said Kirsten. 'We need to follow them, though.'

'All of us?' asked Macleod. 'Why now? Why all of us?'

'Because there's two of them, Seoras. If they split up, I can't follow both. You'll have to follow one of them.'

'Which one?' asked Macleod.

'I'll tell you at the time. I'll work out which one's more dangerous.'

'What's your thoughts at the moment?' asked Macleod.

'I've watched Ricci all day. He doesn't look that dangerous. And I have no idea about her. I've sat and watched her eat dinner. I'll tell you when I know,' said Kirsten.

They watched as Ricci and the woman left the restaurant

CHAPTER 19

and came over towards the park. Remaining in the trees, they maintained their surveillance on the couple as they walked further into the park. Kirsten slowly followed them, keeping Macleod back at a distance because he wasn't the best at sneaking around. But eventually, she allowed Susan Cunningham and him to catch up.

Macleod looked through the bushes and then pulled away, turning to look at Kirsten.

'Do we have to watch this?' he said under his breath.

'You don't have to watch, but it's interesting, isn't it? How did we get to this stage? They looked like they were having a business transaction,' said Kirsten in a hushed tone.

'No, they're having sex. Maybe you read it wrong. Maybe they are just lovers.'

'If they're lovers, why are they not going back to bed somewhere?' said Kirsten.

'I'd be pretty hacked off if somebody took me to the park after dinner,' said Susan.

'Whatever happens?' said Kirsten. 'Don't move.'

'What's going to happen?' said Macleod, ignoring the groans that were coming from several bushes away.

'Just do as I say,' said Kirsten.

Eventually, the couple were dressed again and were making their way back along the path. The next moment they broke apart, Ricci going back towards the restaurant, and the woman walking off in a different direction.

'Which do I follow?' asked Macleod.

'Follow her,' said Kirsten.

'Why her?'

'Instinct,' said Kirsten, and walked after Ricci.

Macleod and Susan Cunningham were at a distance from

the woman. She seemed to walk off in a cheery tone, but then she stopped. The woman doubled over and fell to the path.

Macleod went to race forward, but Susan grabbed his arm.

'It could be a trap,' she said, but Macleod was off. He wasn't holding back. The woman was down and in trouble and he would help. As he got there, the woman didn't move. He slapped her on the face, shook her, but again, there was nothing from the woman. Reaching to find a pulse on the neck, and then on her wrist, he could find none. He looked up at Susan Cunningham, who had arrived, swinging along on her crutch.

'She's dead,' he said. 'She's dead.'

'Say again, Seoras?' It was Kirsten in his ear.

'Kirsten, she's dead. She just dropped onto the—'

'Get out, get out quick! said Kirsten. 'Follow me!'

Chapter 20

Macleod scrambled along with Susan, getting as far away from the dead woman as possible.

'I don't like this,' Macleod said to Susan. 'It's just so quick.'

'You mean you're in the dark?' said Susan. 'It's not like an investigation, is it?'

'No,' said Macleod. 'It doesn't hold back. I've had rough times before. Very rough times. I've had my life threatened, but this is like a roller coaster. It's—'

'Keep going, Seoras,' said Susan. 'Keep going. Come on!'

Macleod realised she was not just keeping pace with him, but was actually quicker. Eventually they saw Kirsten Stewart up ahead who was about to come back out of the park. Macleod saw a sign for the Metro across the road.

'You two, get back home,' said Kirsten. 'Ricci's the key.'

'That woman's dead,' said Macleod.

'I know,' said Kirsten. 'That was a business transaction. He's closing something off. Maybe he's spooked. It's two days to go to the big event.'

'Less than that,' said Susan.

'Exactly. Maybe she had a part. Maybe he's closing the loop,' said Kirsten. 'I'm going to need to stay on him. He's just gone for the metro. I'll follow. You get back to our digs. I'll contact you as soon as I know what's going on.'

'So, all the way back to run out again,' said Macleod.

'In fact,' said Kirsten, 'borrow the car.' She threw keys in Macleod's way. 'It's red. Far side, round the corner. Seoras, you get it and pick Susan up so nobody can see her leg.'

'Why have we not used this car before?' asked Macleod.

'I just acquired one today,' said Kirsten.

'Kirsten?'

'I've got to go.' She tore off over the street, heading for the Metro.

Macleod looked at Susan who gave him a nod, and remained inside the park, under the trees. Macleod strode off to get the car. As he walked round the corner, he pressed the button on the keys and saw the hazard lights of a car light up. He went up to the side of the car, opened the door, and realised he was on the wrong side.

He turned around and got into the other side of the car. It was one of those without a keyed ignition. You just had to have the key on you.

Press start. At least he thought that's what it said. It was in Italian. He pressed the clutch down with the button and on came the lights on the dashboard. The engine opened up. Macleod thought to himself, *not left-hand drive. I need to be on the right side of the road. Left-hand drive, right side of the road.*

Slowly he reversed out onto the road, thankful there wasn't that much traffic. By the time he pulled by to pick up Susan, he thought he was probably on the right side of the road. She jumped in and Macleod drove back to where their digs were.

It was nighttime, and he was having trouble navigating.

CHAPTER 20

Fortunately, Susan was able to point out various landmarks that she'd noted on the way there. So when they arrived back at their digs, she told Macleod to park it several streets away.

'Why?' he asked.

'Because if they find the car, they'll find us.'

'Why are they going to find the car?' he said. 'It's Kirsten's car.'

'She's got it from somewhere.'

'It'll be a Service thing. They won't know it. They won't be able to identify it.'

'It won't be a Service thing,' said Susan. 'She's operating independently. She doesn't want to talk to the Service.'

'Well, how's she going to get a car then? She'll hire it.'

'She will not have a hire car, will she?' said Susan. 'Where's the keys?'

Macleod pulled the keys out of his pocket and handed them over to Susan.

'Look at the bottom,' she said. 'Do you recognise that address? On the tag?'

'No,' said Macleod.

'Of course not. It's because she's nicked it.'

Macleod's face went sullen. 'I'm driving around in a stolen car,' he said.

'Seoras, we just saw somebody die.'

'I can't be—This is—'

'Go, park the car,' said Susan, 'then back to the house. Okay?'

'Do I bring the keys back with me?'

'Where else are you going to put them?'

He shook his head, leaving Susan on the pavement, heading for the house. He drove the car somewhat quicker, and parked it several streets away, before almost fleeing in a furtive manner. *This isn't police work, this isn't right,* he thought. *What sort of world did I send her into?*

* * *

Kirsten Stewart was comfortable with intrigue, comfortable being under pressure and out of her depth. At the moment, she was in a foreign country, following an inspector of the police, and had let her former boss drive off in a stolen car. That didn't matter though. What she needed to do was to keep on Inspector Ricci.

The Metro took him across the city before he jumped on a bus, and then he got a tram out to the suburbs. The night was rolling on into the early hours of the morning. It was one o'clock when Inspector Ricci pitched up at a cafe bar.

Through the window, Kirsten could see him meet with a smart, tailored young man and an older man. Kirsten walked past, turned her jacket inside out to its other reversible side, and then pulled a hood up on her top. She walked inside the cafe bar, ordered a coffee, and sat down in the corner. She pulled her phone out in front of her and kept pressing it, but her eyes were flicking up, constantly watching the three men.

Ricci was talking, but she couldn't hear him. The smart, tailored young man was bothering her. He was in his early twenties. His physique was splendid. His chin was chiselled, and he was clean-shaven. Immaculate, almost. The older man, however, was in a suit and tie with an air of trying to look smart, but in every other regard hadn't seemed to care about it.

Ricci and the older man did most of the talking, the young man just sitting there. Not quite smiling, but never a scowl, either. He gave a nod twice. Kirsten thought about what she was seeing.

Why was Ricci meeting with these people? The young man clearly wasn't in charge. He was taking orders. But he was dressed so smart. And it wasn't the type of outfit you'd be wearing to go out with a woman. It said business. All business. The other man's clothes said boss.

Ricci suddenly stood up, and the younger man got up with him, leaving the older man within the cafe. Kirsten finished her coffee quickly, and then pocketed her phone before moseying her way out the door, never once looking at the older man.

Something inside her was becoming unnerved. *A young man that doesn't speak. That's a man who takes orders. The older man is giving the order*, she thought, *but the young man's gone with Ricci. Ricci must need him for something.*

Kirsten pursued the men as they jumped on board the tram heading back into the city. Sitting at the other end of the tram, she watched them closely from under the hood of her top. When they stood up to get off, she got off at the rear of the tram, keeping a distance between them. When they turned down an alley, she stopped short, instead turning back and circumventing round to find the alley they'd gone down from another angle.

She was sitting down by a wall when they walked out of that alley, into another alleyway at the back. Kirsten had her knees pulled up tight, shivering as if at the back end of a drug dose, and watched as the two men walked past. They didn't bat an eyelid at her, and she was up on her feet, tailing them again.

Ricci cut back down one more alley, and as Kirsten went to peer round it, she halted. There were several men around the doorway. Trouble was, they were hovering there. Why?

In terms of an alleyway, it was nothing. Why would you be here, at this time of night, hanging out? You'd go inside, have a drink, you'd go to the bar. You'd go to a cafe. But here were four grown men, dressed fairly smartly, hanging outside the doorway.

Was the younger man in the cafe part of the criminal underworld? thought Kirsten. *Was Ricci having somebody held here? It made sense, didn't it? It made sense that Ricci, having given over a captive to the gangsters, had then gone to ask for permission to put them down.*

The young man was a specialist. He was there to see it was all done right, if not to do it himself. He was a clean-up man. There was one door and four men. Kirsten picked up her phone and called Macleod and Susan.

'I'm glad you've called in. I've just been in the *stolen* car, parking it up,' said Macleod.

'Get back in the stolen car and get it over here,' said Kirsten, giving her the address. 'Susan will guide you. There's four men outside,' said Kirsten. 'I'm going to draw them off and then I'll get inside. You two can come in with me. Be careful. I think there's a hitman gone in, a clean-up man. Matteo could be in there. Ricci's in there too. Get close, but do nothing unless you have to. Just watch the door. I'll be back.'

Kirsten closed the call and stepped forward into the alleyway. She pulled down her hood and shouted, 'Got a message for you boys!' in French. She lifted her middle digit up, waving it at them. She saw the men become enraged, and one of them ran after her.

Kirsten turned and disappeared back out of the alleyway. One, that was good. He came round the corner ten seconds later, and was grabbed by the throat. His head bounced off a

CHAPTER 20

wall, and then he was dumped back out towards the alleyway.

She heard the feet of the others coming after her. She legged it further down the alleyway she was in, enough so they would see her, and she could draw them away. It would be up to Macleod and Susan to get inside.

* * *

Reluctantly, Macleod got back in the car, and picked Susan up from the flat.

'We need to get going. She's asked for us to help. Matteo—'

'Just a moment,' said Macleod. 'I've still got to drive properly. We're on the wrong side of the road.'

'Clarissa wouldn't have this problem,'

'Don't,' said Macleod. 'The way she drives, the whole of Rome would be on top of us. Stick out like a sore thumb.'

The drive was not far, and soon Macleod had parked up and the pair of them were heading down an alleyway.

'It's round here,' said Susan, swinging along on her crutch.

'She'll be just behind us,' said Macleod. 'We don't need to go in. I think she's wanting us to watch the—'

'I don't care. Matteo's in there. We need to help him.'

Before Macleod could stop her, Susan Cunningham was off, up to the door that Kirsten had indicated to them.

"Wait,' said Macleod, but his words were lost. He tapped on his earpiece. "She's gone inside,' said Macleod.

"What?' said Kirsten. "Get her out! Get her out!'

Macleod took off as quick as he could and burst through the swinging door. He saw Susan ahead of him and grabbed her, pulling her into a room at the side, which fortunately, was empty.

'What are you doing?' he whispered. 'We have to slow down. We don't know what's in here!'

The door out to the alleyway closed behind him. Macleod watched as a figure passed by the open door of the room he had pulled Susan into. He hunkered down in the room's corner, encouraging Susan to do the same. It was harder for her without half her leg, but she was strong.

'Kirsten didn't mean us to go in and rescue him. She meant us to watch in case he disappeared. In case they took him somewhere else.'

'He's got to be in here.'

Suddenly, someone was walking out in the hall. Macleod looked through the small gap in the door from the room. He thought he saw Ricci's suit, the one he'd been wearing earlier on in the evening. There was a man with him. He was pushing another man in front of him. A fourth man brought up the rear, said something to them in Italian and then closed the door.

'What did he say?' whispered Macleod to Susan.

'He said he'd tell the boss it was all being dealt with.'

'Did they just take Matteo away?' asked Macleod. 'We need to get after him. We need to—'

'Come on,' said Susan, pushing up on her crutch to get herself up to her full height. Macleod approached the door, peered out of it, but couldn't see anyone. Carefully, they walked to the front door, opened it and closed it quietly behind them.

'Where'd they go?' asked Susan. Macleod ran down to one end of the alley while Susan hopped up to the other.

He turned and waved at Susan. 'Down here,' he said, 'down here.' Susan swung down. As she got closer to him, she whispered, 'This leads down to a river. I'm not sure how much is occupied down here.'

'Somewhere quiet,' said Macleod. 'It makes sense.' Macleod whispered into his earpiece. 'They've gone. They're on the move.'

'Follow them,' said a breathless Kirsten. 'Follow them. I'm with you. Call out your route. I'll be right behind you.'

Macleod nodded to Susan, and together they followed down the alleyway, keeping to the dark places, hoping that those ahead wouldn't turn round.

Chapter 21

Macleod was not a man accustomed to fear. At times in his life, he thought he was losing his mind. Some cases he'd been in had driven him to a nervous anxiousness. But here, he was out of his depth. This wasn't what he did. He followed procedure mainly. He had a way and a method. Deploying his troops, he was in charge. He sat back and used his brain.

Yes, sometimes he'd run around. He got involved, but these people, they were here to kill you. He had dealt with the Glasgow underworld, and that had been tough enough. But he'd always been on the right side. Now, he was the one who shouldn't be here. He was the one out of place, and yet he knew a man up ahead had his life in the balance.

That man was a police officer, albeit from a different country. And it was this thought that was keeping Macleod going, this thought that allowed him to forget how he was doing this.

Beside him, Susan Cunningham was having no such problems. Her entire thoughts were for Matteo. And to a point, Macleod thought she was actually enjoying it. The rushing around, the intrigue. While Macleod was still thinking about another dead body back in the park, Susan halted. Still a fair

CHAPTER 21

distance back from the small party that walked up ahead, but they'd seen them turn into a building.

Even though it was nighttime, Macleod could tell that the building was half gone, crumbled down and broken. Beyond it, he could hear the river, whatever type of river it was. He didn't know where he was, except in Rome. Rome had been built around rivers, hadn't it? Seven hills? Seven hills and rivers. Tiber. Was that it? He really should have looked everything up before he arrived. He would have done so if he hadn't been so worked up over Susan. Having given himself the task, he should have prepped himself, but he'd run off, desperate to catch up on her. And his mind had been full.

'We need to go in, Seoras,' whispered Susan.

'I agree,' said Macleod. 'Kirsten said she'd be here, said she was coming.'

'Might not have enough time,' said Susan.

Macleod looked behind him. He'd called out his route.

'Where are you?' he said, before his breath was gone.

Kirsten came back to him, 'I'm on my way. I've just finished with them.'

Macleod wondered what finished with them meant. It wasn't something that she was used to saying, because there'd been that slight hesitation before she used the word finished. Had she despatched them? This side of Kirsten was causing him problems but he had to admit she was what kept him alive in all of this craziness.

'We're going in,' said Macleod. 'He may not have time to wait for you.'

'Don't. I'm on my way,' said Kirsten.

Susan shook her head at Macleod and pointed to the building. She would not take no for an answer, and started swinging herself across on her crutch. Macleod followed her to the door. As they got there, he peered around the edge into the darkness.

The night was dark amongst the alleyways, but here the open roof of the building had opened up to the moonlight, which shone down. Matteo was standing, his hands tied up behind his back, facing away. Macleod noted that Ricci was there, standing to one side. The young man in the smart suit was also there, preparing what looked like a weapon. But there was another man, too. He was big, broad-shouldered, but looking away from Macleod. Macleod looked around him. On the ground was a large stone, about the size of a palm.

'What do we do?' said Susan. 'We've no weapons.'

Macleod looked inside again. The new man, possibly a guard, had a gun. Macleod could see that. Yes, his suit jacket was over it, but Macleod saw the distinctive outline.

'Make a distraction. I'm going to get the gun off that guy.' Susan stared at him. 'I can run and overcome him,' said Macleod. 'You distract them, and I'll be able to do it.'

Susan looked at him once, looked inside at Matteo, and then swung herself in on her crutch. She cried out in Italian. Macleod, seeing all eyes turned towards Susan as she got clear of the doorway, stole in quickly and cracked the additional guard across the back of the skull with a rock. As the man went to tumble forward, Macleod pulled out his gun and turned to point it at Ricci.

'I didn't think you'd have it in you. And this lady. I like this lady,' said Ricci. 'Half a leg missing, whizzing around the place. You walked into the trap set by our double tail though, didn't you? You walked into the trap, and you came out of it. I was wondering how. Working together, I see,' said Ricci.

'Everybody put their guns down,' said Macleod.

CHAPTER 21

'Making demands now. Is this how you do it back in good old England?' said Ricci.

'Scotland,' said Macleod. He hated how everyone referred to the UK as England.'

'You may not realise it, but you're in Rome now. Macleod, isn't it? Obviously didn't fall for my little message.'

'I worked in Glasgow,' said Macleod. 'Rome won't have anything on Glasgow.'

Ricci laughed, reached inside, and pulled out a gun of his own.

'You get many guns over there. No? The UK is so civilised that way, isn't it? Few guns. You don't arm all your police officers.'

'Neither do you,' said Macleod.

'No, but I take my own precautions,' said Ricci. 'And this man over here. Well, he's not on the force, is he?'

'So you let the criminal world hang on to Matteo, in case they got caught, so you could deny it was you,' said Macleod.

'You're catching on, Inspector,' said Ricci. 'I heard about you. They said you were shrewd. Old. Not that dynamic anymore. But shrewd. Clever mind. Where's the other one? I was hoping you'd send the other one over.'

'I sent you our best.'

'You sent me a cripple,' said Ricci. Susan was standing in between Macleod and him. The man in the smart suit had a gun pointed towards her.

'You need to put down your weapon,' said Ricci. 'You need to put it down or my friend will kill Detective Constable Cunningham.'

'I put it down and you'll kill both of us. And Matteo Lombardi. You're after one of your own. You're going to despatch one of your own. There's nothing worse than a dirty cop,' said Macleod. 'That guy there,' he said, pointing at the hitman. 'He, I understand. He's just part of the filth. You, you're worse than it. You pretend to be something you're not.'

Macleod wasn't one for talking, but currently he was holding a gun and having guns held back at him. Kirsten had said she was on her way. She was the ace in the hole. She was the one who could come in and save him. He wasn't sure if he fired, if he'd still be standing by the time that bullet had hit Ricci. Even if he could hit Ricci.

Macleod didn't use weapons. He had never fired a handgun in his life. Sure, he'd been in court, he'd heard all about them, how they work, what people did with them. He would just pull the trigger, wouldn't he? But he had no experience of them, none whatsoever.

'What's it gonna be?'

'Detective Macleod. Chief Inspector. I hate to say it, but to get caught over here, so out of your depth, international incident, bit of an eponymous way to end a career.'

'I am not going anywhere,' said Macleod. 'Not today.'

He looked across at Susan. She was shaking, no longer enjoying the ride. Who could blame her with a gun pointed at her? Her bravado had got her into the room. It had got Macleod over the threshold. But in truth, what was he going to do?

He hadn't worked that bit out. He'd thought pointing the gun at Ricci might have made him stand down, but the man was holding a gun at him. To fire would be suicide.

Macleod would get a shot off first, surely. He glanced at Susan. She was trying to give him some sort of faint smile, as if to say it's all right. Almost acceptance, and yet her body was

CHAPTER 21

shaking with it.

Macleod swallowed. He could feel his own legs beginning to tremble. Could he even get two shots off in time? Could he save her? Should he turn round and fire first at the young man in the suit, and then whip back to Ricci? Maybe he would shoot him first and then—no, because even if he hit him, Ricci would shoot Macleod, and Susan was standing there without a gun. It was a no-win situation. There was nothing here. He might take Ricci on the way out. Or he could give up, but that meant certain death.

Macleod squeezed the gun hard into the palm of his hand. He felt his finger on the trigger. He looked at Ricci, and with a sudden short move, pulled the trigger back.

He'd expected the kick, the gun to ricochet up after the shot. He'd expected his ears to ring loudly with the gunshot, but there was nothing. The trigger didn't go the whole way. The mechanism failed. And he saw Ricci laugh.

'You don't use guns very often, do you, Detective Chief Inspector?'

I was right there, thought Macleod. Had he missed something? What had he missed?

'It helps if you take the safety off,' said Ricci.

Macleod dropped the gun down to look at it. Where was the safety? What was the safety? He knew Ricci was still looking at him.

'Well, you made a mess of that, didn't you? Too bad. I'll despatch you and then, we can interrogate your friend. Find out just what she does know before we kill her. I'll bury her with Matteo. After all, the two of them were very close.'

Susan spat towards the man, but he raised his gun again, towards Macleod.

'Goodbye, Inspector.'

Macleod braced himself for the impact from the weapon, but as he did so, there came a sound of feet bursting into the room. Then there was a gunshot, but he felt no impact. A second shot followed it, incredibly close, but slightly different in how the sound reverberated off the walls. There followed a third and a fourth shot. Macleod couldn't feel a thing.

His eyes had involuntarily closed at the sound of the first shot, and his hands reached to his body, but there was no pain. He opened his eyes.

Across the room, Inspector Ricci lay dead on the floor, blood was pouring from his head. He swung around and looked over at Susan Cunningham, who was standing on her foot, trembling. Beyond her, the smart suit of the man was covered in red.

Macleod looked behind him.

'I said don't go in,' said Kirsten Stewart, 'and now we need to get out of here, fast. That man over there,' she said, pointing. 'Is that Matteo Lombardi still facing the wall? Is that who we came for?'

'Yes,' said Susan, swinging her way over towards him.

'Then get hold of him and let's go. Back to the digs.'

'Shouldn't we do something with these bodies?' asked Macleod. 'Put them—'

'That sound's going to bring everybody running here. Seoras, I just shot two people. With me quickly until we get out of here.'

Macleod forced his legs to turn and follow Kirsten Stewart back out of the building. She tore down through alleyways, asking where the car was. Without a drop in pace, Kirsten routed them back there. Eventually, all four were inside

CHAPTER 21

driving through Rome. Macleod sat in the front seat, staring ahead.

He wondered at first, was it the shock of the impact she had made? Was it seeing Ricci's body? Was it thinking he was dead, expecting the impact of the bullet? Were those things making him shake?

Then he realised he had been prepared to kill. He was going to take down Ricci. It was only the safety on the gun that had stopped him. He glanced across at Kirsten. She turned momentarily, gave him a nod, and then a half smile.

'We're out the other side,' she said. 'We'll be okay. Don't worry about it. The fact you couldn't do it. The fact you couldn't fire,' she said. 'It's a line when you cross, you don't come back from.'

He nodded, but turned back, looking ahead as the streetlights of Rome passed by him. He had crossed that line, but God stopped him from going too far. Leaving the safety on. Or had he just made a terrible amateur mistake? Either way, he realised whatever else happened, he wouldn't be as innocent ever again.

Chapter 22

Macleod sat on the sofa in the Italian flat hideout that Kirsten had established. Beside him, looking with concerned eyes, was Susan Cunningham. Matteo was badly shaken up and there were bruises on his face. No doubt there were more over his body. Macleod had made himself useful and was bringing in coffee and some food for everyone to eat, while Kirsten Stewart sat in the single chair opposite the sofa.

'So fill us in,' said Kirsten, 'from the moment you were taken captive. Susan sorted out all before that for us.'

'I was grabbed,' said Matteo. 'I was blindfolded. We didn't leave Rome. We never travelled far enough in a car to do that. I was then taken into a room and left there for a couple of hours. When they came back, I was tied to a chair. At that point, they asked questions and tried to illicit answers. Most of them kept their faces covered, at least that first time. It gave me the impression they were city gangsters,' said Matteo.

'Recognise any of them?' asked Macleod.

'Not then,' said Matteo, 'but I was blindfolded initially.'

'After questions?' prompted Kirsten.

'The first twenty-four hours or so, it was the same people,

CHAPTER 22

and then someone else came in. That was when I saw Ricci.'

'Must have been before we got to him,' said Kirsten.

'He had a story invented about me and Susan. Told everyone we were off on an affair, said that it was over for me, unless I talked. But I didn't. It would have been over for me anyway, until you came,' said Matteo. 'But the evidence is locked away.'

'Evidence?' said Macleod. 'We found some of it in your house.'

Matteo looked shocked. 'But that was hidden.'

'It was hidden pretty well,' said Kirsten. 'But for someone of my ability, it wasn't hidden well enough.'

'Are you from the police as well?' asked Matteo.

'She's not,' said Macleod. 'She doesn't exist. Okay? We don't talk about Kirsten after this.'

'Whatever,' said Matteo. 'And you're Susan's boss?'

'I'm Macleod. I'm the one that Ricci contacted initially. And I sent Susan over. I'm actually her boss's boss, but let's not get caught up on it. More importantly, you said that you saw some of them. Did you recognise any of them?'

'I knew at that point I was in trouble when I started being shown their faces. The ones I saw were low level. At first, I thought they might be former Mafia Capitale, but I think they're Camorra. I recognised a few of their faces.'

'Camorra?' said Macleod.

'Originally from Naples. Now have criminal operations in Rome,' said Kirsten. 'Mafia Capitale was an organised crime network exposed in 2014. But I thought they'd gone away, so you might be right with Camorra.'

'I recognised some faces. Locals. But there was another one there that surprised me.'

'Who?' asked Kirsten.

'Benedetto Bianchi. I've seen him at the station. At least that's the name he goes by. But he's not a police officer. He comes in on certain meetings. Usually high up meetings, private meetings. Ones you don't get invited to unless you're well in the know. I think he's from another department.'

'And he's different from the others?'

'Yes, Kirsten,' said Matteo. 'Very different.'

Susan Cunningham reached up and stroked the side of Matteo's face. He winced, pulling away first.

'At least they didn't get you,' said Matteo. 'Who knows what they would have done to you?'

'They're just lucky I've lost a leg. If I had two good ones, I'd have taken them on.'

'I'm at a bit of a loss as well,' said Kirsten. 'I don't know how I would fight these people.'

Macleod raised an eyebrow. 'You seem to have done pretty well with it.'

'I do what I have to when I have to, Seoras. And yes, it's blunt. But you don't solve problems with your fists. You solve them with your brain. Who taught me that? Who taught me to think? That's why they wanted me in the Service. They would have wanted you as well.'

'Would have. You're guessing now,' said Macleod.

'Well, actually, they wanted you. I know that for a fact,' said Kirsten. 'What they didn't like was your moral stance. You weren't ambiguous enough for them.'

'And you are?' asked Macleod, with an accusing tone.

'No, I'm not. And I don't work for them anymore.'

'Who are we talking about?' said Matteo.

'It's not important,' said Kirsten. 'What is important is Benedetto Bianchi. How do we find out who he is? Do we

CHAPTER 22

have enough evidence to talk to your bosses, Matteo?'

'The evidence is circumstantial. There's nothing one hundred per cent concrete. We've also got the problem that this big event is happening soon. Sorry, I've not kept track of days. Is it over? Are we—'

'It's going to happen in less than a day's time,' said Macleod.

'Even if we go to the right superiors, and I don't know which ones to go to,' explained Matteo, 'it would be too late by the time they act on it. It would warn everybody off, anyway. Either that, or it'll push them into doing it quicker.'

'So how do we go at it?' asked Kirsten.

'Think about it,' said Macleod. 'Benedetto Bianchi is not known to Matteo, except by face. He doesn't know who he works for. But the man's in top meetings. So, he must work for the government, at some level. Either that, or he's working for somebody with deeply private interests, who's close to government. Now I'm not sure that's the case. Police forces don't like that. And as corrupt as you can be, you still have to work within one that isn't corrupt. Especially to be so open, to be about the place. If he was truly on the wrong side, or meant to be on the wrong side, they would meet more discreetly. And his face wouldn't be known.'

'What are you saying, Seoras?' asked Kirsten. 'What are you getting at?'

'What's the face I would have seen if I'd been in Matteo's position back in Inverness? Not necessarily trusted, but at least would be on our side.'

'You're not suggesting,' blurted Kirsten.

'I know you've left. I know you've walked away, but I haven't. We need to reach out to Anna.'

'Anna?' said Susan. 'Is that the one you were talking about

before?'

'Anna Hunt,' said Macleod. 'Kirsten's former boss.'

'Who does this Anna Hunt work for?' asked Matteo. 'I'm confused.'

'Anna works for the clandestine services. We call it the Service in the UK.'

'Anna doesn't work for them,' said Kirsten. 'She is them. But I don't know her allegiances anymore. I don't know how it all stands,' said Kirsten. 'There were issues.'

'Issues aside,' said Macleod, 'won't she have connections with the Italian Service?'

'She has connections in lots of Services,' said Kirsten.

'Well, we need to flex those connections and make them work for us. We need Anna to talk to her Italian counterparts and see who Benedetto Bianchi is. And now Anna is top level, it's even better. We don't want to be hitting a mid-level who could be involved. How else are we going to see who's involved in this? How are we going to track down Bianchi?' said Macleod. 'We're talking a potential hit here.'

'You pulled me in to extract Susan. I've done that,' said Kirsten. 'Matteo's life was at risk. We've done that. Throw it all at the Italians and let them deal with it.'

'It won't get dealt with in time,' said Matteo. 'Please!'

'Kirsten,' said Macleod, 'the whole time I've worked, it's been about the ones in trouble. You know that. Someone is on the end of this, in trouble. Someone is going to get killed during this *significant event*. We need to get there. We need to try.'

'She's spoken to Hope before, hasn't she?' asked Kirsten.

'A few times,' said Macleod.

'Right then. Tell Hope to get a hold of her.'

'Will she know how?'

CHAPTER 22

'If Anna's spoken to her before, she'll know how. You know that, Seoras.'

He looked across at Susan Cunningham who was sitting with her mouth wide open.

'Did we just not see this stuff at Constable level?'

'No,' said Macleod, 'you don't.' He picked up his phone and placed a call to Hope McGrath back at the Inverness station.

* * *

Hope was agitated. Macleod had sounded edgy. It had been quiet at Hope's end; very quiet. There was occasional contact from Macleod's Garda friend over in Ireland, who said Jane was fine. She was anxious, worried, but no wonder. She would have had no contact with Macleod either; neither had Hope. Not until the call to contact Anna Hunt.

She remembered meeting Anna Hunt, for the woman unnerved her. And that wasn't easy to do with Hope. Hope was taller than most women, at six feet. She was fit, agile, and strong. And Hope could handle what most people threw at her, in terms of barbs from their words.

There wasn't much that Hope feared, but Anna Hunt put her in a state of unease. You're never sure where the woman was coming from, when she was going to arrive. And when she did, she looked so slick and professional. You got the feeling you were an amateur. Anna wasn't young either. She must have been heading towards her fifties, if not already there.

Hope left her office desk, and made her way to the lady's washrooms. After concluding her business there, she walked back along into the office, and Ross stopped her.

'Got a phone call up from down below. There's a PC West

looking for you. In the canteen.'

'PC West? West? Never heard of a PC West,' said Hope.

'Neither have I,' said Ross.

'Did they say what it was about?' asked Hope.

'No, offered nothing. I said they could just come up and meet you, but the person said they were in the canteen, as they needed to get some lunch, said they might be an old friend. The front desk wasn't that clear on just exactly who they were.'

'I'll pop down and see them then,' said Hope.

Hope took the stairs at a slow pace, wondering who this could be. Would it be a contact? Was this Anna Hunt's way of getting through to her? Send in a random constable from somewhere to talk to her. Seoras had sounded urgent in his request and Hope felt uneasy. Something was up, she was sure of it. But she didn't know any detail at all.

Hope swept into the canteen and looked around her. She saw several familiar faces from Uniform. But in the corner, in the depths of the canteen, was someone she didn't know. The shape looked wrong. And then Hope clocked what she was looking at. The constable had her face away from Hope, turned slightly, as if she was looking at something. But when she swung back, there was a very faint smile and a nod.

Hope walked up to the canteen hatch, asked for two coffees, and then took them over to the table, putting one down in front of the PC. She was smaller than Hope. Significantly so, but she gave off that aura of professionalism.

'Nice uniform,' said Hope. 'You joining us?'

'I thought it best not to come up to the office. People talk, don't they? Also, you said that Macleod felt it was urgent. By the time I'd set up a meeting out at Loch Ness, or wherever else, time would be against us.'

CHAPTER 22

'Shall I tell you what's been going on?'

'No,' said Anna. 'Susan Cunningham went to Italy to assist with a potential murder investigation. Suspicious death, anyway. While out there, she told Macleod that she had thoughts it might be murder. Susan apparently has done a runner with a Matteo Lombardi, a superintendent out there, and they've disappeared off in a car, ready to cause a right scandal. Susan's also the one that lost her leg.'

'It's not very Susan,' said Hope.

'Suddenly, Macleod goes on a holiday to Ireland,' continued Anna. 'Been big on Ireland for a while, has he?' Hope gave a small grin. 'Out in Ireland, his partner Jane is having a wonderful time, but he's not there. He's in Italy.'

'How do you know that?'

'I don't know he's in Italy, just surmised it. What I do know is he's not in Ireland. I checked.'

'I got a message from her,' said Hope. 'On her private phone saying she was in trouble. That's why he went. He felt that if he made it official—'

'He felt that if he made it official, she could get killed. And he didn't contact me because . . .'

Hope stopped for a minute. She was ready to speak. Ready to tell Anna what she knew, but then she stopped, thinking about it again.

'Ah! That's why,' said Anna. 'He's got Kirsten involved.'

Hope just raised her shoulders. 'I don't know how much to tell you,' said Hope, 'if I'm being honest with you. I didn't know about Kirsten at first.'

'You've told me enough. Kirsten wouldn't have come to me as she doesn't work for me anymore. Kirsten would have gone out to handle it. But if Macleod's talking to me now, well,

Kirsten's at an impasse.'

'Apparently, they've got hold of Matteo and Susan. But something big's happening. It involves a person called Benedetto Bianchi.'

'Benedetto Bianchi,' said Anna quietly to herself. 'One moment.'

She took a mobile phone out of her pocket, stood up and walked over to the window of the canteen. Hope couldn't hear what she said, but she returned two minutes later.

'Benedito Bianchi is Italian Secret Service. Similar to our MI5. If I'm being asked about Benedito Bianchi, it's because they're not sure of him. Kirsten's going to need help. If it's gone like this, it's not about police investigations anymore. Maybe not even about simple corruption.'

'Macleod said there was the possibility of an organisation carrying out something serious. He was worried we would be overheard, or the phone be tapped.'

'I doubt it. Kirsten would have given him a clean way to contact you. Contact him back. Tell Kirsten to contact Emanuel.'

'Is that it?' asked Hope. 'Is that all?'

'How long have you known me?'

'For about five minutes total,' said Hope. 'We met on occasion, but I don't know you.'

'No, you're right. You don't, do you? How long have you known Kirsten?'

'I used to know her. Before she left to go to you.'

'She's not the same person who left,' said Anna. 'Tell Kirsten to contact Emanuel. And as for me, what I will do with what you've told me? Trust that I will do everything to resolve this situation.'

CHAPTER 22

Hope picked up her coffee, finished it, and then stood up.

'I know it's hard when you're not in control,' said Anna Hunt. 'I spent my life trying to maintain control. But you get through in this place because you trust each other. I get through in my job by keeping secrets and knowing who to trust and when. Kirsten has come to me. Macleod has come to me. They know who to trust and when. So, trust me too, Hope.'

Hope gave a nod, turned, and walked out of the canteen. Anna Hunt finished her coffee, stood up and walked out of the station to the car outside. Once inside the car, she picked up her phone and called her base.

'Get me everything we've got going on in Italy at the moment, specifically around Rome,' she said.

'You heard something?' said a voice at the other end.

'You could say that,' said Anna. 'You could say that.'

Chapter 23

'What is this place?' asked Macleod. It was a back street in Rome, a dusty, bleak sort of shop that didn't seem to have too many people in it. A woman in the front sat in a chair, crocheting. When the door opened and Macleod and Kirsten entered, she looked up, but that was all.

'This is the place you come to when you need to know what's going on,' said Kirsten.

'Why didn't you think to come here?' asked Macleod.

'This is the place Italians come. You don't just walk in uninvited. They know we're here. They know why we're here. That's why we're just walking in happily. Pick something up over there and have a look at it.'

'Why?' asked Macleod.

'Keep the pretence up. You never know who's watching.'

'Is somebody going to meet us then or speak to us?'

'They will do,' said Kirsten. 'Or at least, I'll get some sort of indication in a moment. But look at something, please.'

'Why?' asked Macleod.

'Seoras, this is the world I work in, okay? Stop asking the questions and just do as you're told.'

CHAPTER 23

Macleod looked at her. It was like the headmaster had spoken. A bell rang from somewhere in the back, and Kirsten looked over at the woman in the chair. She was old, probably in her eighties, but she was sharp. As soon as Kirsten looked, the woman showed with her eyes that Kirsten should go through to the rear of the building.

'Come on,' said Kirsten.

'What?' said Macleod.

'We've just got the go-ahead.'

'Where?' asked Macleod.

'Trust me. Follow me.'

Kirsten walked through to the rear of the shop, pushed aside some beads that hung from the lintel of the door. In the back, a man was sitting, playing cards.

'Hello,' he said in Italian. And Kirsten said hello back. She asked if they could speak in English, for her partner wouldn't be able to understand the Italian. And the man nodded.

'You must be Stewart,' the man said. 'And this is Macleod.'

Macleod looked nervous about his name being known. 'And you are?' he asked.

'Emmanuel,' said the man. 'Benedetto? Someone said you had concerns.'

'Yes,' said Kirsten. 'Do you?'

'Unsure,' the man said cryptically. 'He's part of Morandi Gallo's crew, but Morandi was waylaid recently—got her leg caught in a bear trap while out in the woods.'

'Is that some sort of code?' asked Macleod. Kirsten shook her head.

'You don't see many of them,' said the man. 'I wonder how she stumbled into it. She's been off since. It's going to take a while to fix up her leg. You need to see Morandi.'

'Address?' asked Kirsten. The man reached into his pocket, pulled out a folded piece of paper, and placed it on the table in front of him. 'Does she know I'm coming?'

There was a shake of the head. 'Be careful.'

Kirsten stepped forward, took the piece of paper, and gave a thank you in Italian to Emmanuel. Macleod went to ask another question.

'Shush,' said Kirsten. 'That's it. We go.'

'But we need to find out more. We need to—'

'He said, Morandi's the person; we have the address, we go.'

'But does his people think there's—'

'Seoras? Go!'

Kirsten strode out of the shop without another word, Macleod following in her wake. Once they were on the street, he turned, annoyed at her.

'What's that meant to mean? What did we get? We got an address to see another person. Are we getting the runaround? He could have told us if they think something's happening. He could have told us—'

'Oh, he did,' said Kirsten. 'He sent this to Morandi. They're not sure if something's up, but they're worried. You don't let an operative from somewhere else charge in. And you certainly don't let an ex-operative from somewhere else.'

'Would Anna have told him you were coming? Told him you'd left them?'

'She will not tell them I worked for them, in case something went wrong. But clearly they're worried. Anna must be worried too, to swing it like this.'

Kirsten opened up the piece of paper in front of her. 'Oh, heck,' she said. 'I'm going to have to get another car.'

'I couldn't just hire one?' said Macleod.

CHAPTER 23

'Seoras! Matteo and Susan are two of the most wanted people at the moment. You will be too. And me. The difference is that they are currently hidden. You and I are out in the open. No damn rental cars!'

'Where's this address, anyway?'

'Not far off the Via Appia, outside the city. Give me ten minutes and I'll pick you up on the corner here.'

Macleod glared at her. 'That easy? You can just do it that easy?'

'I've had a bit of practice, Seoras,' said Kirsten. 'We're under the cosh, Seoras. I don't just steal cars every day for no reason.'

Macleod wasn't happy at all. It was a petty crime. Low-level crime, but it was still a crime to grab a car. He was struggling to come round to that view that Kirsten had, that the bigger picture needed served, so she just did what she had to do. Maybe that's why they didn't want him. But they'd looked at him, and there was a sense of pride in him—but also a sense of horror. Was it really something he should be delighted about, that they thought he could be this type of character?

The drive out on the Via Appia was a relatively quick one, and as they turned into countryside, Kirsten found the address with ease. She drove up the driveway to what was a rather elegant looking house. As she parked the car, she turned to Macleod.

'Do nothing to provoke her,' she said.

'We're going to see someone with an injured leg,' said Macleod.

'We're going to see someone that's close to the top of the tree in their Service. There are cameras watching us at the moment. I'm coming in like this, so she knows I'm not a threat.'

'What do you mean, she knows you're not a threat? Why

would she think you're a threat?'

'Trust me. Don't make any rash movements. Don't question her intensely. Okay?'

They got out of the car and walked up to the front door, pressing on the doorbell. The door opened with no one there. Kirsten stepped in, but Macleod looked a bit bemused.

'You just follow me,' said Kirsten. A decorative hall led through to a living room with an enormous fireplace on one side and a chaise-longue that had a woman in shorts and a t-shirt sitting on it. Her leg was out in front of her and it did look sore.

Kirsten stood for a moment as she entered and assessed the woman before her. She had long white hair, and looked to be somewhere in her fifties or sixties. Kirsten noted she was in trim shape apart from the leg being damaged, but she also had piercing blue eyes.

'I'm not carrying anything,' said Kirsten, opening up her jacket. 'I'm not here for—'

'I didn't think you were here to assassinate me,' said the woman, 'and why would you bring an old man with you?'

'This is Detective Chief Inspector Seoras Macleod of Police Scotland. He works for our police service.'

'And why is he with Kirsten Stewart, formerly of the UK Service.'

'I'm with him actually,' said Kirsten. 'Susan Cunningham, one of his constables, came over to help with a routine investigation into a death in the Colosseum. British tourist. She worked with Matteo Lombardi.'

'Well, they've run off together. I don't do fetch jobs like that. Why would you come here for that?'

'They didn't run off. They were taken underground and held.

CHAPTER 23

Matteo Lombardi thinks that there's an organisation seeking to put certain individuals at the top of police, civil, and church organisations. He thinks there's a hit happening soon.'

'Do I look like someone who can help?' said the woman. 'I'm out of it. I'm out of it for another month or two and I'm quite enjoying it.'

'Emmanuel has sent me to you,' said Kirsten.

The woman suddenly sat up more formally. 'Why?' she asked.

'Benedetto Bianchi. Matteo Lombardi thinks Benedetto is corrupt. He knows he comes into the station but he was also there when Matteo was being tortured after being captured.'

'How do they say in your country? Bullshit,' said Morandi. 'If he saw his face, he'd be dead.'

'He was taken out to be killed. I got to him and saved him.'

Morandi shifted uncomfortably. 'Was Benedetto there?'

'No. He left it for some goons.'

'Well, that's a pity. You've given me no evidence. All I've got is Lombardi's word. Emmanuel didn't contact me either.'

'No. Ricci, Matteo's boss, is also dirty. I've been following him. He despatched a woman in the park, recently. Something is up. Someone in Italy is going to be taken out within the next twenty-four hours or so. And, frankly, we need to know who or why. But Benedetto has got something to do with it.'

'I'm not telling you anything. I'm not telling you what my boys are doing. You've given me nothing. Nothing to say this is genuine. You're not even in the Service anymore. We collaborate. We share information. But not with you. You're outside of the Service.'

'Does she know your number?' asked Kirsten.

'Of course she knows my number.'

Kirsten nodded, picked up her phone, turned her back, and walked away for a moment.

'What's going on?' asked Macleod.

'Out of your depth, are you? Be careful following her. They say she turned the Service inside out.'

'Kirsten?'

'Yes,' said Morandi.

'Kirsten was in the police with me. There is no one finer than her.'

'You don't have to lie here. You don't have to—'

'I'm not lying,' said Macleod. 'You don't know me and this is not what I do. I'm a detective chief inspector. I don't play these games. I tell you now, I wouldn't be here if I didn't trust her.'

The phone beside Morandi went off, and she picked it up.

'Long time, no hear,' said Morandi. Kirsten had returned and was now standing beside Macleod, a faint smile on her face.

'Who's with her?' asked Morandi into the phone. 'Describe him.'

Kirsten looked a little on edge. Macleod was bemused. Who was on the phone?

Morandi put the phone down a few moments later, picked it up again, and dialled a number.

'Anna Hunt says this is genuine. We need to move on it, though,' said Morandi.

She turned away again, intent on the phone call she was making. But she didn't speak to the phone and neither did Macleod hear anything coming back to her. For the next five minutes, she tried calling, and then she put the phone down. She turned back to Kirsten and Macleod.

CHAPTER 23

'Benedetto is organising the protection of the Pope when he speaks in St Peter's Square. There's no response,' she said. 'He's running a level of protection where the people guarding around his Holiness don't even know they're there.'

Macleod saw Kirsten's face give a look of horror.

'Can you get more of your service there?' asked Kirsten.

'Benedetto will see them. He'll know they're coming. I'll try to make arrangements.'

'And I need to go,' said Kirsten.

'Have you anything concrete on this? Have you anything more than just Matteo's say?' asked Morandi. 'Hard evidence to go through?'

'Not right now,' said Kirsten. 'We're going.'

'Can't she contact him?' blurted Macleod. 'Morandi, can't you contact your people? Tell them to call him off. Tell them to—'

'He's operating in the dark,' spat Kirsten. 'They won't see him. They won't know where he is. And he'll recognise them. The people he won't recognise is you and me.'

'You'll need to be quick. He's speaking in a couple of hours, at most,' said Morandi.

Kirsten ran for the car. Macleod stood for a moment, looking back to Morandi and out where Kirsten had gone.

'Well, go, Inspector,' said Morandi; 'go!'

Macleod ran out of the door, got into the car, and Kirsten spun it round on the driveway quickly.

'Well, Seoras. You said you wanted to save someone. Today's your lucky day!'

Chapter 24

'How do we get in, past those running protection for the Pope?' asked Macleod. 'That is where we're going, isn't it? It is the Pope?'

'Yes,' said Kirsten. 'What we don't do is go in where the crowds go. The weather's getting ridiculous as well.' She looked at the thermometer on the car. 'It's through the roof, Seoras. Get a hold of Matteo.'

Macleod put a call through to Susan Cunningham's phone. 'Ask Matteo what's going on with the Pope. He's speaking in St. Peter's Square, but the day is scorching.'

'It'll take place inside, he says,' replied Susan Cunningham, after a moment. 'The heat will be too much.'

'Is it a full-on public address?' asked Macleod.

Again, after a moment's hesitation, Susan replied, 'No, but they'll move inside. So, it'll be in the Paul VI Audience Hall. It's a smaller gathering; not a public one. He's addressing parts of the Catholic Church, according to Matteo. But they'll have a top layer of protection around him.'

'Why?'

'Matteo says because of certain elements. Within the crowd, there'll be certain factions, people from various criminal

CHAPTER 24

organisations.'

'Why?' said Macleod.

'Because like anywhere, isn't it?' said Susan. 'The people who run a lot of these organisations try to present themselves as good citizens on top. They're obviously worried about his Holiness, being so close to them.'

'Great,' said Macleod. 'That's all we need.'

'It makes sense though, doesn't it?' said Kirsten. 'Why the others were involved. Why they would have a criminal element taking care of Matteo. If you're going to put people in the right place, there's got to be payback right down the line. That's what's going on here. But that's up to the Italian authorities to sort out,' she said. 'We've just got to stop it from happening, then get out.'

'What do you want me to tell the other two?' asked Macleod.

'Tell them I'll pick them up in fifteen minutes. To be ready.'

'You sure it's wise for us all to go? Maybe you should go on your own,' said Macleod.

'They've got a full set of protection around him. Protection you won't see. I'll be fully pressed just to make an impact. You guys could get there. You're the ones they won't suspect, and the ones who'll have a chance. Seoras, this could go very wrong. We might not pull this off. I know you look at me at times and what I do. But trust me on this one; I'm up against it.'

'How do we get in?' asked Macleod.

'Catering. There's always catering. And the people that do the catering are not always known,' said Kirsten.

'But Susan's got half a leg missing. How's she going to get in?'

'Beggar. She pulled it off with that beggar stunt. She needs to do something similar. Tell her she's got ten minutes to come up with an idea and get herself dressed.'

By the time they had picked up Susan Cunningham and Matteo, Susan was half-wrapped up in what looked like a massive Indian sari. She had ripped down curtains from part of the hideout, and flung them around herself. The wild and decorative style seemed to work, as well as wrapping something around her head. She looked almost foreign, despite her pasty-white, Scottish features.

'We go in through the back. We'll make it about catering. Food choices,' said Kirsten. The route into the Paul VI Audience Hall would be a torturous one. Security will be tight, but there is always the possibility of getting through. There are always back routes for catering and ancillary staff.'

'How do we do this?' said Macleod. 'How do we know where to go?'

'You will not like it?' said Kirsten.

'Why?' said Macleod.

'We're going to have to put pressure on somebody innocent to get us in.'

Having picked up Matteo and Susan, Kirsten parked the car up near a set of large kitchens. Catering was always done in these places and the people that did it were never big and well-known. Just workers. Those who serve, those who give out food, they look like anyone, and they usually changed rapidly. Nobody wanted to do this as a career, not unless you were the chef or working at the high end of it.

Kirsten disappeared from the car and came back ten minutes later, ushering the three of them into a building at the side. As Macleod stepped through the door, he saw three people on the ground.

CHAPTER 24

'You didn't?'

'No, I didn't,' said Kirsten. 'These are just people going about their job. They're out cold, but we get changed into their outfits.'

Macleod saw the serving attire, and without embarrassment, Macleod and Kirsten changed.

'Make sure you clip the passes on and don't speak except in Italian,' said Kirsten.

'But I can't speak Italian,' said Macleod.

'Then don't speak,' she said. 'Susan, you're going to be talking to me about allergies. You're going to be talking to me about problems with food. Okay, and we just keep marching forward. Once we're inside, I will grab someone, and they will lead us through to the hall.'

The four left the room heading towards the kitchen area, which was thoroughly busy. Food was going to be on offer after this meeting and there were entrees for beforehand. Kirsten waited until they pushed through a kitchen area into a small alcove outside. A young man was standing there, looking slightly bemused.

Without hesitation, Kirsten grabbed him, put a hand over his mouth, and pushed him roughly up against the wall.

'Have you been here long,' she said, in Italian. The man nodded. 'Do you know how to get to the Paul VI Audience Hall?' The man nodded again. 'Do you know how to get there by the back way? Not the way most guests would take?' Again the man nodded.

Kirsten pressed something into his back that Macleod couldn't quite see. 'You take us there or you're dead,' she said in Italian. 'Now walk us there quickly.'

As they walked, Kirsten whispered to her hostage, 'This talk the Holy Father's giving in the audience hall, has it started?' The man nodded. 'Then walk quickly,' she said.

They marched along several corridors, until they got to one where Kirsten could see two men in suits on the door. The man halted.

'It's along there and beyond,' he said. 'We are not allowed that way yet.'

'How far are we from the hall?' Kirsten asked.

'Through that door, keep following it round. There's a door off to the right that you would enter the hall through. There's also a viewing hatch further along.'

'A viewing hatch,' said Kirsten. 'How big?'

'Big enough to look through. Not much more. Very discreet,' he said. 'It's so we know when they're coming out. When we need to have the food ready. We can see what's going on without being in the hall.'

'I want you to turn away from me now and go back the way you came. And go home,' said Kirsten. 'Don't come here. Don't shout at anyone. Don't raise the alarm. If you do, I'll come for you.'

The man nodded, and Macleod could see him shaking as he walked away. 'What did you tell him?'

'Told him to go have a lie down,' said Kirsten, smiling. She then turned and started walking up the corridor towards the two men who were standing in the hall.

In Italian, Kirsten announced to them, 'We need to get this representative into the hall. She's lost. She's come the wrong way.' Kirsten pointed at Susan Cunningham in her foreign attire.

'You can't come this way,' the man quickly said back in Italian. Kirsten continued to walk forward, dragging Susan

CHAPTER 24

Cunningham with her.

'She's got mobility problems,' said Kirsten. 'This is the quickest way. We can go through here.'

'You can't come this way,' said the man. Kirsten was now within six feet of him and continued to walk forward. The men raised guns in front of her. 'Whoa,' said Kirsten.

'You can't come this way. Take her the other way. You cannot come through here. You cannot!'

Kirsten got to a foot from both men before she swung up, knocking one gun out of one man's hands and him off the wall. Kirsten's other hand grabbed for the other man. His hand holding a gun, had his wrist twisted violently, and the gun dropped. Kirsten grabbed both men by the head, knocking them together. She then brought one head down to her knee, smashing the face hard, before she turned and put a sleeper hold on the second man.

Thirty seconds later, both men were lying on her feet.

'They're not dead, are they?' asked Macleod.

'Not yet,' she said. She reached down and picked up both guns, putting them inside her pockets. 'This way. Quick,' she said. She turned to offer Macleod a gun, but he shook his head.

'Never used one. Never want to use one.'

Once through the doors, Kirsten raced up the corridor, Macleod and company following behind. She took a right, going out of sight. As Macleod got to the turn in the corner, he heard the commotion beyond. Quickly, he glanced round.

Kirsten was in the middle of five men, fighting hard in the corridor. She was getting held and hit. Beyond them, Macleod could see a man on the end of a tall stilt. He was looking through a small scope. This was it, the assassination attempt.

The shot must have been reasonably far, because as far as

Macleod could tell, it was a quality rifle that the man was using. As he rounded the corner, some of the men engaged with Kirsten shouted at him. He saw one man about to grab Kirsten from behind, and Macleod charged forward, jumping on him from behind.

The man instantly threw Macleod off his back onto the floor, and the inspector hit the ground hard. Bending over, the man rained a blow onto Macleod, but Kirsten kicked his chin, knocking him backwards.

'The gunman, you need to stop the gunman,' said Kirsten, and then her voice was gone. She was hit from the side and was pinned by two men, a third man battering into her. Macleod became engaged with one on the ground.

Matteo ran forward to grab hold of a fifth man, but the man had raised a gun. Matteo was shot in the shoulder and was knocked back off his feet. Susan Cunningham had thrown the sari off, her crutch and leg now exposed. She swung hard towards the crowd.

Kirsten managed to get an arm free and had grabbed the wrist of the man who had fired the shot, twisting it so violently that Macleod could hear a crack. The gun dropped. Kirsten kicked it up the hallway beyond the group. Beyond them, the man with the rifle got round behind it, preparing to shoot.

One of the men went for Susan Cunningham and Macleod, still on the floor staving off one man and his back in agony, swung a leg, tripping the man as he went to intercept her. The man tumbled and Susan brought her crutch down on his neck, skipping over him. She dived forward, grabbing his gun in front of her, now fallen to the floor.

'Shoot him!' shouted Kirsten. 'Don't think, just shoot!'

Susan reached down, picked up the gun and pointed up the

CHAPTER 24

hallway. She fired once and a light fitting exploded beyond the rifle man. She fired five more times. He spun off at one point, tumbling to the floor and then doors were opening everywhere.

There was mass panic from inside the hall. Chaos reigned. Macleod was picked up, and held in place by two police officers. Someone recognised Matteo, but first aiders were now running in. Gradually paramedics arrived.

Someone was watching Macleod, guarding him. All he could do was sit where he had been deposited, his back sore, his mind reeling. He looked over at Susan. She had thrown the gun once she'd shot the man. And for that, Macleod was grateful. If they'd come out armed with guns and had seen that Susan was armed they may have shot and asked questions later.

The lights in the corridor were off and on, and everywhere Italian was being spoken, leaving Macleod out of the loop.

He looked around for Kirsten to help. This was her world. She would know how to clean this up. She would know what to do. And then he realised she wasn't here. How was she not here?

He was hauled to his feet and taken away, escorted by two police officers. They had at least the decency to handcuff Susan to a police officer while she used her crutch to walk. Matteo went away on a stretcher. Now the consequences would be faced, he realised. But he smiled to himself. Susan was alive. He was alive. Kirsten was who knew were. And just maybe, he'd done a good thing. He only hoped they would recognise it.

Chapter 25

Macleod stepped out of the car and felt the wind on his face. It was the west coast of Ireland and, in typical fashion, you could see the rain clouds some way off, rolling in towards the beach. They would be here in half an hour, maybe less.

The sunshine wasn't particularly strong but it was refreshing after the heat of Italy. He walked around the rear of the car, opened the door and let Susan Cunningham out. She swung along on her crutch, seemingly happy. Well, no wonder, after all they'd gone through.

'Do you want me to wait, Inspector?' said a voice.

'Just to make sure she's in,' said Macleod. 'If she's in, it won't be a problem. When you say she's been okay—'

'She's been fine,' said the Guarda officer. 'Absolutely fine. I'm not sure she's been out much. I didn't see her down the pub, anyway, more's the pity. If you're staying, you can come down and see us. We'll line one up for you.'

Macleod nodded, aware of what the man meant. There was a music-filled pub near to the coast. They lined the pints of Guinness up, preparing them as they went along, letting them settle when half-filled before nearly filling them and then

CHAPTER 25

topping them off. There was such an order for Guinness that it kept going through the night.

'I'll wait here,' said Susan. 'Probably best you see her first. She'll want to throw her arms around you.'

'I haven't spoken to her since I left. I'm more likely to get a slap to the face,' said Macleod with a smile.

But he was keen to see Jane again. He forced himself not to skip his way in, finding the front door open. That wasn't particularly unusual in this part of Ireland. He searched through the house, and her clothes were here, but she wasn't. When he got to the kitchen, he saw a note saying she was having a picnic. The place she'd indicated was less than half a mile away. Macleod came back out.

'Fergus, if you don't mind, can you run us down the road? She's having a bite to eat, apparently.'

'Well, it's not a bad day for it. But she'll have to get her backside in gear. I think the rain will come soon. Although, it showers most of the day.'

Macleod nodded and got back into the car accompanied by Susan Cunningham. Fergus drove them down the small country roads with the stone fences encompassing green fields.

This was the Ireland that was talked about. The countryside that Fergus reminded him of when he met him at policing conferences. It was some time since, but they had remained good friends, and now the rental house Fergus had provided had been ideal for Jane. Having someone to look in on her and make sure that she was safe was even better.

Fergus parked the car up and Macleod could see Jane at a picnic table some five hundred yards away. There was another person with her, although Macleod couldn't tell from this angle who it was.

'I'll hang back,' said Susan.

'Don't be ridiculous,' said Macleod. 'She's got somebody with her anyway. You'd better come with me in case they're violent.'

Susan started for a moment, but then saw Macleod's face and gave a laugh.

'Thanks again, Fergus. I see she's got a car now with her.'

'Any time, Seoras,' he said. 'She's been fine. I've checked in on her. I think the other guy's been watching as well.'

Macleod looked over at him. 'The other guy.'

'Aye, it's all right, he's one of ours. In the general sense.'

Macleod was a little bemused, but he walked over towards where Jane was sitting, hearing Susan swinging her leg behind him. He sat down beside Jane straight away and she hugged him tight.

'So you've come back,' she said.

'Aye,' said Macleod. And he turned to face the woman opposite. Alone, black hair down either side of what looked like a weary face. It was a beautiful face, though. *Older beauty, though*, thought Macleod. One of those faces that didn't age with time. It had seen a lot, and at the moment, it wore a faint smile on the lips.

'Detective Chief Inspector,' said the woman. 'Your good lady seems to have enjoyed herself.'

'Thank you,' said Macleod. 'This here,' he said, pointing to Susan, 'is Detective Constable Susan Cunningham. Susan, this is Anna Hunt. She's the—'

'She's a friend. I am somewhat aggrieved though,' said Anna. She was wearing a black bomber jacket. Macleod had seen she'd had blue jeans on with boots.

'I understand that. A friend of mine here says that Jane was

CHAPTER 25

well looked after, not just by Fergus. So, thank you.'

'DCI Macleod disappears quickly for a holiday in Ireland and then vanishes. Of course I'd put somebody on to look after her. Besides, she's very engaging, Jane. We've been having a delightful conversation about you.' Macleod looked a little bit awkward. 'Oh, don't worry. She's very faithful. If you don't mind, Jane, I could do with a word with your husband. Business. I'm sorry.'

Jane said, 'of course. I'll just take a walk over by the way.'

'Susan,' said Macleod. 'Why don't you talk to Jane for a bit?'

'What, let the grown-ups deal with this?' she said.

'It's a good job we're not back at the station because that sounded very insolent,' said Macleod. 'But we're not, so yes, let the grown-ups talk.'

Susan hopped her way over to Jane, and Macleod heard a rather disconcerting laugh between the two of them, before he turned his attention back to Anna Hunt.

'The Italian Service are thrilled with your efforts. Very happy. Good job too, because you went to their patch and operated without their knowledge.'

'I'm sure it wouldn't be the first time someone's done it.'

'No, but we wouldn't have blundered in like you did,' said Anna. 'I'm also aggrieved that you went to Kirsten, not me.'

'Susan's special,' said Macleod. 'She's one of mine. I needed someone who was going to go for her. Not someone who would have other agendas.'

'A very accurate assessment,' said Anna. 'But she was a British citizen. I would have gone for her and got her. But I understand.'

'And Kirsten tells me she doesn't work for you anymore. I thought there would have been much more communication, much more a nod and a thanks. Less official looking than a DCI and someone who is now the head of the Service.'

'I will not confirm or deny rumours like that,' said Anna with a smile. 'Kirsten may not know what she's talking about. She's not with us. I would suggest that you reach out to me for matters of national interest.'

'That's understood,' said Macleod. 'But the Italians are all happy.'

'The Italians are not all happy,' said Anna. 'One of their Service tried to take out one of the top leaders in their country. I'm sure if he knew what had happened, he'd thank you greatly. It would be a good thing too. All that press. Protestant from the Western Isles saves the Pope. Although you'd probably get a bit of flak from some of your church people. And his church people would complain, too. Still, at least you're putting all that past behind you, aren't you? Or are you?'

Macleod gave her a stare. 'I may not be the man that I once was, and I don't have problems with other people's religion.'

'Lighten up. I'm just messing with you,' Anna said. 'But on a serious note, where's Kirsten?'

'I don't know,' said Macleod. 'When we were in the corridor, and Susan tagged the shooter, so to speak, everybody rushed in. Kirsten vanished.'

Anna smiled. 'Of course she did. You see, it's one thing having a DCI go across and bravely try to help his constable. It's an easier story to tell. You'd uncovered a whole trail, but Kirsten was not someone that needed to be there. As a spy, you can't be seen to be doing that. That's the difference. Don't think you'd have liked that if you'd joined us. That's why we never asked.'

'You nailed that one on the head,' said Macleod. 'And I don't

CHAPTER 25

know where she is. She hasn't spoken to me. And if she did, I wouldn't tell you. In fact, I wouldn't tell you. She would tell you if she wanted you to know. And if you were really desperate, you'd come and get it out from me. But tell me,' said Macleod, 'the Order of Calgacus, is it being dismantled?'

'Morandi Gallo, the woman you visited, the woman who you advised her subordinate was part of this Order, what did you make of her?'

'She's not that different from you.'

'No, she's not. And if her subordinate has been part of this Order, she is ripping him up, left, right and centre. I heard Matteo is heavily involved with her now. He was quite something, and she was impressed by him. I think Susan was, too.

'Morandi said that I should do something for Susan. She can't help her directly because Susan's over here. But I think Susan will find out that the prosthetic that she's waiting on will arrive a lot sooner than she's expecting. I'll let her know. I've put her up in a hotel in town before she flies back up. You and Jane have another week here.'

'I haven't booked it for that.'

'No, you haven't. I've booked it. Enjoy yourself. Next time, come to me. I'm your friend,' said Anna. 'I know you look at us and you think about our agendas and that, but Susan is a British citizen and one of ours. Hamish Ferguson was one of ours. We'll investigate and find out. Don't go charging across into a foreign country again. You'll only get yourself killed. You've got the brain, but you haven't got—'

'I haven't got the skills that Kirsten has. And, this is not for repeating to Jane, Anna, but if she hadn't been there, I'd have been dead within twenty-four hours of arrival.'

'At least she called somebody,' said Anna. 'Time to go back home after your week off, and get on with cleaning up Scotland. It's what you're good at. You're good at bringing the rest of them on. Do that. Contact me if there's anything beyond.'

She stood up, walked round the table, and put her hand out to Macleod.

'Take care of yourself, Inspector. Good job. Bad way of going about it.'

And with that, she was off, heading towards Susan Cunningham. Shortly, Jane came back over and sat down with Macleod. They watched as Anna departed with Susan. Jane threw her arms around Macleod.

'Are you okay?'

'Sort of,' he said.

'But Susan came back.'

'She did. I saw somebody else out there, though. Didn't realise what I'd done for them.'

'Oh,' said Jane. 'In a bad way.'

'I really don't know,' said Macleod. 'I saw a different life out there. It's not one for me.'

'Anna says that we're getting a week's holiday in one of the top hotels near here. That's nice, isn't it? You never told me we'd won something.'

'Must have slipped my mind,' he said. Macleod picked up his phone and snaked an arm around Jane. 'We're having a week's holiday,' he said. 'A proper holiday. You and me. You deserve it.'

He winced as he held her tight, bruises smarting across his chest. She wouldn't ask about them, but she'd wonder. He knew that. He heard the call connecting.

'DCI Hope McGrath.'

CHAPTER 25

* * *

'Oh, hello, Seoras,' said Hope, sitting in the canteen. 'I've just popped down for a snack. You're back?'

'I'm back in Ireland. I'm having another week off. Jim will probably know about it.'

'Didn't you tell him?'

'Somebody will have told him. You've got the fort, okay? Much happening your end?'

'No. Other than meeting your friend, nothing. It's been quiet. I hope it stays that way for a week.'

'Susan will be back up with you in a couple of days. She might want a few days off herself. She's going to have some good news coming about her prosthetic. So, you need to work out when that's getting booked in as well. How's Ross?'

'Oh, still bitching about what time he can get off to see his kid. Not happy you just swanned off, either. Felt that was inappropriate, and you just took a holiday when he fights for his.'

'As long as you didn't tell him.'

'Of course I didn't,' said Hope. 'As long as you're okay.'

'We are. I might tell you the tale someday. Maybe.'

'Well, enjoy your holiday,' said Hope. She closed the phone call and put the phone away in her pocket. Looking around at the uniformed constables about her, she realised she might have been having a quiet week, but policing went on whatever day it was.

Hope sighed, stood up, and returned her coffee cup to the trays sitting in the metal tray rack. She climbed the stairs up to the office and gave a nod to Ross at the back and Perry sitting behind his computer, as she walked to her own office.

She opened her door, closed it behind her, and sat down. Only when she was sitting in her chair did she notice that somebody was in the far corner of the room. They were quiet and motionless. They weren't on a seat, but were sitting down against a wall. Hope wouldn't have seen them, not until she got into her seat and sat down. Even then, she only saw the top of their hair.

'Hello?' said Hope.

'Brought the old man back for you,' said a voice. Hope's heart leapt.

'Kirsten?' she said. 'Kirsten Stewart. What the hell are you doing here? You're meant to be—'

'Brought the old man back,' she said again.

Kirsten stood up. She was wearing blue jeans, a tight crop top t-shirt and had a bomber jacket on. She walked over to Hope.

'Brought the old man back for you. He needs a week off. Couldn't handle the heavy going.'

'You still with them?' asked Hope.

'I'm on my own,' said Kirsten. 'And you are in here. This was his office.'

'It was. . . . Moving up though. What about you?'

'Had a rough time,' Kirsten said to Hope. 'Fell in love. He broke my heart. Went away to find myself. Helped out an old friend and thought, what should I do? I'm thinking of coming back, back to the homeland. Back to Scotland.'

'Inverness?'

'I don't know. Somewhere. Somewhere close to here. This is home. I think it's time I came home.'

'Back with us.'

'No, I can't go back to being an officer,' she said. 'I don't know what I'll be doing. But I'll be about. Anyway. Macleod told me you're happy now. Got a man. Got a run of any car you want.'

Hope laughed. 'I have to joke about John running a car hire firm. I am happy though. Detective Inspector McGrath, by the way. And are you happy?'

Kirsten Stewart shrugged her shoulders. 'Not yet. Getting there, though. I'm getting there.'

Read on to discover the Patrick Smythe series!

READ ON TO DISCOVER THE PATRICK SMYTHE SERIES!

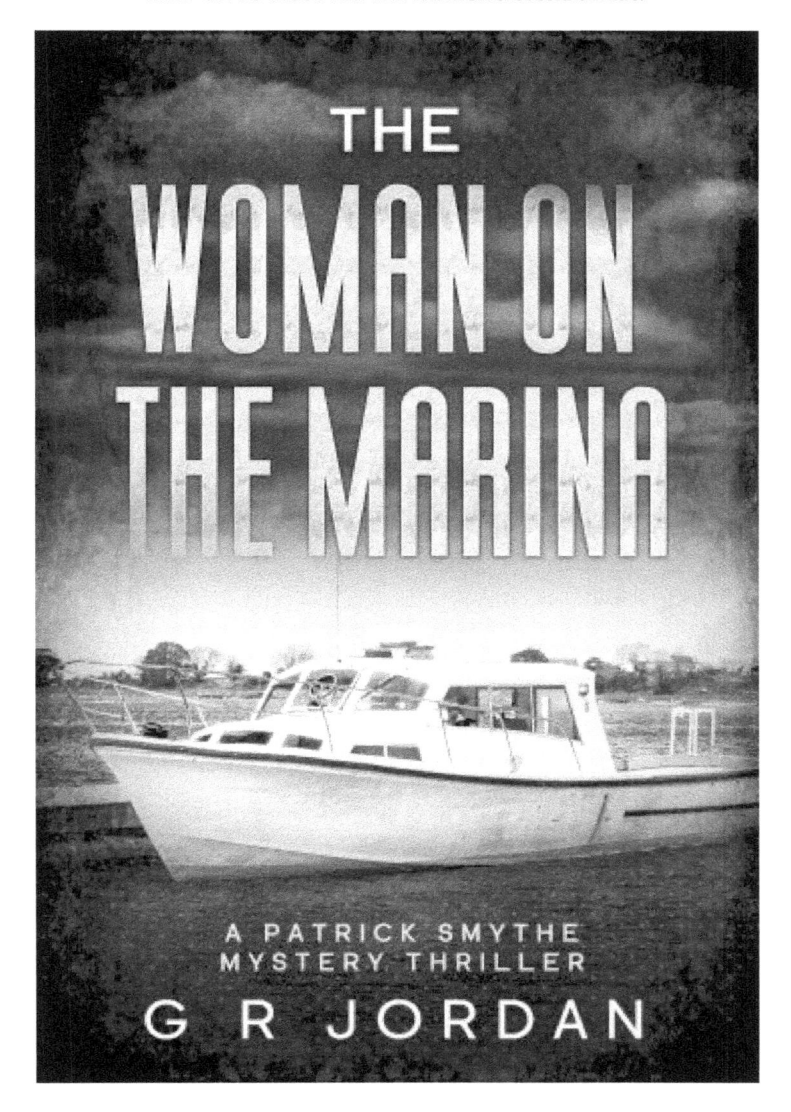

THE WOMAN ON THE MARINA

A PATRICK SMYTHE MYSTERY THRILLER

G R JORDAN

Patrick Smythe is a former Northern Irish policeman who after suffering an amputation after a bomb blast, takes to the sea between the west coast of Scotland and his homeland to ply his trade as a private investigator. Join Paddy as he tries to work to his own ethics while knowing how to bend the rules he once enforced. Working from his beloved motorboat 'Craigantlet', Paddy decides to rescue a drug mule in this short story from the pen of G R Jordan.

Join G R Jordan's monthly newsletter about forthcoming releases and special writings for his tribe of avid readers and then receive your free Patrick Smythe short story.

Go to https://bit.ly/PatrickSmythe for your Patrick Smythe journey to start!

About the Author

GR Jordan is a self-published author who finally decided at forty that in order to have an enjoyable lifestyle, his creative beast within would have to be unleashed. His books mirror that conflict in life where acts of decency contend with self-promotion, goodness stares in horror at evil, and kindness blindsides us when we at our worst. Corrupting our world with his parade of wondrous and horrific characters, he highlights everyday tensions with fresh eyes whilst taking his methodical, intelligent mainstays on a roller-coaster ride of dilemmas, all the while suffering the banter of their provocative sidekicks.

A graduate of Loughborough University where he masqueraded as a chemical engineer but ultimately played American football, Gary had worked at changing the shape of cereal flakes and pulled a pallet truck for a living. Watching vegetables freeze at -40'C was another career highlight and he was also one of the Scottish Highlands "blind" air traffic controllers.

These days he has graduated to answering a telephone to people in trouble before telephoning other people to sort it out.

Having flirted with most places in the UK, he is now based in the Isle of Lewis in Scotland where his free time is spent between raising a young family with his wife, writing, figuring out how to work a loom and caring for a small flock of chickens. Luckily, his writing is influenced by his varied work and life experience as the chickens have not been the poetical inspiration he had hoped for!

You can connect with me on:
- https://grjordan.com
- https://facebook.com/carpetlessleprechaun

Subscribe to my newsletter:
- https://bit.ly/PatrickSmythe

Also by G R Jordan

G R Jordan writes across multiple genres including crime, dark and action adventure fantasy, feel good fantasy, mystery thriller and horror fantasy. Below is a selection of his work. Whilst all books are available across online stores, signed copies are available at his personal shop.

A Time to Rest (Highlands & Islands Detective Book 38)
https://grjordan.com/product/a-time-to-rest
A luxurious spa on the Isle of Harris becomes a hotbed of suspicion. The star therapist is found dead in a seaweed wrap. Can DI Hope McGrath unmask a killer hiding behind a façade of island tranquillity?

When the lead therapist of an exclusive wellness resort is discovered murdered, DI Hope McGrath must navigate a world of alternative therapies and hidden agendas. As the team delves deeper, they uncover dark secrets beneath the serene surface of this Hebridean retreat. With suspects ranging from jealous staff to troubled clients, can Hope restore balance and bring a killer to justice?

On this tranquil isle, some come to heal, others to hide their sins!

Kirsten Stewart Thrillers
https://grjordan.com/product/a-shot-at-democracy
A luxurious spa on the Isle of Harris becomes a hotbed of suspicion. The star therapist is found dead in a seaweed wrap. Can DI Hope McGrath unmask a killer hiding behind a façade of island tranquillity?

When the lead therapist of an exclusive wellness resort is discovered murdered, DI Hope McGrath must navigate a world of alternative therapies and hidden agendas. As the team delves deeper, they uncover dark secrets beneath the serene surface of this Hebridean retreat. With suspects ranging from jealous staff to troubled clients, can Hope restore balance and bring a killer to justice?

On this tranquil isle, some come to heal, others to hide their sins!

Jac's Revenge (A Jack Moonshine Thriller #1)

https://grjordan.com/product/jacs-revenge

An unexpected hit makes Debbie a widow. The attention of her man's killer spawns a brutal yet classy alter ego. But how far can you play the game before it takes over your life?

All her life, Debbie Parlor lived in her man's shadow, knowing his work was never truly honest. She turned her head from news stories and rumours. But when he was disposed of for his smile to placate a rival crime lord, Jac Moonshine was born. And when Debbie is paid compensation for her loss like her car was written off, Jac decides that enough is enough.

Get on board with this tongue-in-cheek revenge thriller that will make you question how far you would go to avenge a loved one, and how much you would enjoy it!

A Giant Killing (Siobhan Duffy Mysteries #1)
https://grjordan.com/product/a-giant-killing

A body lies on the Giant's boot. Discord, as the master of secrets has been found. Can former spy Siobhan Duffy find the killer before they execute her former colleagues?

When retired operative Siobhan Duffy sees the killing of her former master in the paper, her unease sends her down a path of discovery and fear. Aided by her young housekeeper and scruff of a gardener, Siobhan begins a quest to discover the reason for her spy boss' death and unravels a can of worms today's masters would rather keep closed. But in a world of secrets, the difference between revenge and simple, if brutal, housekeeping becomes the hardest truth to know.

The past is a child who never leaves home!

Milton Keynes UK
Ingram Content Group UK Ltd.
UKHW040637131024
449481UK00001B/15

9 781912 153527